TALLAHASSEE LASSIE

PEG SUTHERLAND

Harlequin Books

TORONTO • NEW YORK • LONDON
AMSTERDAM • PARIS • SYDNEY • HAMBURG
STOCKHOLM • ATHENS • TOKYO • MILAN
MADRID • WARSAW • BUDAPEST • AUCKLAND

Published October 1992

ISBN 0-373-25514-4

TALLAHASSEE LASSIE

1

"WAKE UP, LAZYBONES. That's sunshine out there, sleepyhead," she said in a low intimate whisper. "Time to pu-u-ull those covers back and stre-e-etch those arms. There. Isn't that better? Mmm. What's that I smell? Coffee?" she purred.

"See? There *is* life before 6:00 a.m.—as long as you're listening to Jammin' J.T. on WFLA, Tallahassee's classic-rock station." Raising her voice, she ordered, "Open your eyes, lazybones! This is your Wake-Up Call!"

Jillian Tate Joyner reached over to plug in a golden-oldie tape cartridge. "Now, how about some rise-and-shine music from Bobby Darin to get you hopping this morning?" she spoke forcefully into the microphone suspended in front of her.

The rousing beat of the rock-and-roll standard "Splish Splash" filled the studio as Jillian busied herself stacking eight-track cartridges for the songs and ad spots on the roster for the next hour.

As she tapped her suede boots to the music, Jillian relaxed somewhat, the butterflies she felt prior to starting her first morning shift on WFLA finally vanishing. Still, Tallahassee was unknown territory. She had to win over a whole new set of listeners—listeners who were itching to turn the dial to another station at the sound of an unfamiliar voice—especially an unfamiliar *female* voice.

Even in the nineties women disc jockeys were about as welcome as women in combat.

But her jitters weren't major. She hadn't spent five years as Atlanta's top morning DJ without gaining a great deal of experience.

"Tallahassee can't be that tough," she muttered to herself as she fluffed out her wild mane of burgundy-red curls around the headset. "Besides, who could *resist* Jammin' J.T.?"

When the music ended, Jillian flipped a switch to activate her mike.

"That's more like it," she said vivaciously. "Amazing what a steamy shower does to rev up the old bod, right, Tallahassee? It's 6:17 on a ..." she continued in a more confidential tone. "Shh, let's keep this quiet—Monday morning. That's right, seventeen minutes after six in the a.m. Plenty of time for a good strong cup of coffee and a quick scan of the morning paper before you hit the parkway."

She stretched and grinned. She was doing just fine. More than fine. Great! Tallahassee was going to be *all* right.

"You're right, radio land, this is WFLA coming at you. And this is Jammin' J.T., your Tallahassee Lassie! A woman on the air. Can you imagine! But who knows, maybe a lady DJ might not be such a bad idea, after all?" She laughed.

"Now, how about a little coffee-brewing music for 6:21 on a ... Monday ... morning. Then we'll take a look at what the weather has in store for us today. How does sunshine and eighty-two degrees strike you? And we'll talk about something I read in the paper this morning. You won't believe what our pals in the state legislature are cooking up now. What a bunch of wild and crazy guys."

She plugged in the next cart from her stack, and checked to make sure the weather report from the newsroom would be ready on time. When she glanced up, she noticed the station manager eyeing her cautiously from the hallway.

Jim Towers was compact, but had a powerful, domineering presence. Most definitely, Towers did not rely on warm fuzzies as part of his team-building strategy.

She bet he seldom rolled into the station at 6:00 a.m.

To make sure he knew how much she appreciated his efforts to welcome her, she raised both arms over her head in a two-thumbs-up salute. She wondered if he was already having doubts about Jammin' J.T. and her leather miniskirts, her inch-long, deep purple nails, and the unkempt curls that were now a different shade of red than they'd been during her interview.

He'll really love the shade I'm planning for tomorrow. Then she winked at him before turning her attention back to the control panel.

"Welcome back, Tallahassee!" she said as the song ended, her heart racing as she anticipated the next segment of her lineup. Her routines with characters she'd created were always her favorite part—a link to the one aspect of her childhood that she remembered fondly. "We're pushing 6:24 a.m.—thirty-six minutes until seven for you pessimists out there—so you'd better shake a leg. Now, I've got someone special here in the studio this morning, for some political commentary. Folks, I'd like to introduce you to Jolene Dellinger, who's made a career out of studying the legislative process—most of it from behind a pair of scissors. Jolene runs the hair salon around the corner from the capitol building, and most of her customers are serving time in the big dome. Welcome, Jolene."

Almost unconsciously, Jillian physically transformed herself into Jolene. She narrowed her green eyes and drew her full lips into a thin, hard line. In a nasal drawl that was nothing like her own voice, she declared, "Well, hello, y'all. Yer right, J.T., they ought to be servin' time. What's that? That's not what you said? Well, never mind. Lemme tell you who came in yesterday to have his roots retouched so he'd look real purty when he stood in front of the rest of the legisla-tors. You know, he had to look purty so they wouldn't pay no attention to that all-fired dumb bill he introduced about jackin' up taxes again...."

Switching quickly back to her Jammin' J.T. voice, Jillian jumped in to interrupt, as smoothly as if there were really two women in the control booth. "Now, hold on, Jolene. I hear some of Florida's poor elected officials barely scrape by. I heard one of them didn't even have a hand-carved mahogany desk yet. Imagine how he feels when the lobbyists come in. Maybe a tax hike isn't such a dumb idea."

"'Not a dumb idea'?" Jolene screeched. Jillian was pleased with the effect. Shrill outrage was a feeling most of her listeners could identify with. Jolene was a new creation, but Jillian already felt she'd known her forever.

"Not a dumb idea, you say? Honey, where you from, anyway? Must be from somewhere out of state, where they spend taxes on good stuff like schools and roads. Shoot, for all the taxes I pay, I figure I ought to be able to drive without rattling my fillings. You know, the dang highway to Gainesville still needs work. How in the world do they expect the Gators to get up here for football games if they don't fix the roads? That's what I want to know. Football games—now that's important. Am I right or what?"

Suddenly another character joined the conversation. Unexpected, yes, but Jillian's characters often exercised more control over her than she over them. At times like this, she could understand why nothing else had ever mattered to her mother. For the first two decades of her life, Jillian had watched her mother being possessed by her characters—on TV, in movies and even at the breakfast table.

The voice of her own new character was silky and sultry. Jillian felt her lids droop; her lips settled into a provocative pout. "Ooh, football. Making the team has been one of my lifelong dreams."

At which Jillian decided she'd better jump in before this latest creation got out of control—the bits of dialogue that were forming in her head would need censoring.

"Now, Jolene, I thought I told you to leave Dixie Rose at home this morning," Jillian chided. "And speaking of teams, the news team's here to fill us in on the headlines they'll be covering on the half hour. Let 'er rip, guys."

Jillian turned away from the console and lifted her heavy curls off her neck. Then she began fanning herself. Creating people was hard work—especially when they came at you so fast you couldn't keep them in line.

Releasing her hair, she sat upright to cue up the next ad spot. Looking out through the glass window into the hall, she saw she'd attracted another spectator—a woman in a dark tailored suit, her briefcase propped on the window ledge. Her dark hair was cut short, conservatively styled, and she wore just enough makeup to

look polished but not glamorous. Jillian assessed her.
The kind of woman who usually took herself too seriously to appreciate Jillian's flippant style or understand
her professionalism; the kind of woman who took *everything* far too seriously. Jillian smiled at her and the
woman straightened her spine almost imperceptibly.

"Keep an eye on the clock, folks, it's moving up on 6:51
a.m., nine before the hour on WFLA with your new Tallahassee Lassie, Jammin' J.T. Jolene'll be back next half
hour to finish her capitol commentary," Jillian promised, not taking her eyes off the woman in the suit. "But
for now, let's take a look at the sports pages in this
morning's *Tallahassee Demogogue*—uh, *Democrat*.
Now, I don't know about you, but when I look at the
sports pages, I'm looking for hunks. Brawn. So what do
I get this morning? Golf. Now, I don't know about you,
but men in lime-green polyester don't stack up next to a
pitcher in those bun-hugging pants. Am I right?"

She looked up in time to catch a smile twitch at the
corners of the woman's mouth before she picked up her
briefcase and walked away.

"Yeah, I thought so. Brawn and buns. A sure winner
every time."

THE LAST INCHES OF the tape ran off the spool and continued to flap on the reel-to-reel. Russ Flynn stared at the
spinning equipment from which, moments before, a
throaty female voice had mesmerized him since the
completion of his own morning shift.

"Holy cow," Tony Covington said, astonished.
"Somehow I wasn't expecting that."

Russ pulled himself up in the lumpy swivel chair and
flicked off the tape.

"I figured she'd be . . . sort of . . ."

"Second-rate? Unentertaining?" Russ's boyish grin transformed his sharply chiseled face. "Not fit to wipe your shoes?"

Tony grinned back. "Yeah. Something like that."

"Guess again, *compadre*. Jammin' J.T. is anything but second-rate."

"You said that, brother. But who expected it? If she's so good, why'd she leave a major market like Atlanta? Doesn't add up," Tony responded, with obvious bafflement.

"Tell me about it. I called our Atlanta station right after 'FLA made the announcement. They said the stories are true—she *was* number one in the morning. And her station offered to double her take-home if she'd stay."

Tony's eyes widened. "So this show's probably no fluke."

"Nope." Russ frowned as he recalled the show they'd just heard. Jammin' J.T. was funny. She had timing. She had a stable of offbeat characters. And a nose for what was hot news.

In fact, she had all the qualities Tallahassee listeners—surveyed by his station—had said they liked about Russ Flynn. All the qualities that set him apart from the typical no-brain record-spinners were qualities that Russ was too burned-out to generate anymore.

"Suppose you've got yourself some real competition this time, brother?"

At Tony's words, Russ felt a flutter of excitement— something else he was also having trouble generating every morning when he faced his console. He would have welcomed excitement—it had been too long since he'd felt any real enthusiasm over being on the air. But he had a hunch that what he really was feeling was something closer to uneasiness.

He grinned reassuringly at Tony. "I can handle it."

Tony threw his head back and laughed. "I hope so. She is one bad mama, Flynn. You catch that bit she did on the governor's new limo? That is one funny lady, my man. First time on air and she already knows who to hit on. The lady has—"

"Whoa!" Russ held up his hands in front of his face. "Let 'FLA do its own promotion, how about it? I'm still the top gun here at WKIX. At least, I was, the last time I checked."

Tony slapped Russ on the knee as he hoisted his stocky frame out of the chair. "You're still the top gun in *town*." He paused at the door and pointed at Russ, shotgun style. "At least, for now. That lady could be bad for your health."

"Thanks for the vote of confidence, *compadre*."

Russ didn't let his station manager's parting words bother him. First he cut a couple of promotional spots for the next day's program, then headed out of the station. *Although maybe they should bother me. If Tony could only read my mind. If he could only sense the restlessness that makes it tough to come into the station every morning....*

But he can't, Russ reassured himself, pulling on his helmet and strapping his sport coat in place behind the seat of his motorcycle.

Straddling the bike, he pushed all thoughts about the station aside and focused on the pleasure of riding. Only when on his motorcycle could he escape, lose himself in the fantasy of being someone stronger and smarter than Russell K. Flynn, Jr.

He remembered the first day he'd ever ridden one—almost twenty years earlier. It was the summer cousin Eugene had worked for the Dairy Dreme and saved up enough to buy a dirt bike, with a slender, shiny yellow gas tank, thick-treaded tires and raised fenders. The machine had fascinated him, but he'd figured he was no match for it—the way he figured he was no match for anything in his life.

But on that bumpy patch of sandy earth north of his folks' farm, Russ had felt power shoot up his arm as he'd twisted the handlebar to rev the engine. The roar had pulsed through him, making him forget that he was nothing but a farm kid with hayseed in his hair and dirt on his jeans. Leaving behind cows that needed milking, hills of beans that needed weeding and geometry notes that desperately needed deciphering, Russ had felt in control of something for the first time in his life. Even when he'd hit that first big bump at the top of the rise behind Grandpa's old house and gone flying over the handlebars, he'd felt more exhilaration than fear.

The sunny day was already heating up as Russ inched the bike through lunchtime traffic. Even the breeze hitting his face and his bare arms below rolled-up sleeves was hot. He felt the mist of perspiration along his hairline. Soon, the asphalt along Tennessee Street would be generating the kind of egg-frying heat that would have him coveting the air-conditioned vehicles he passed.

Russ drove his motorcycle into the parking lot of an athletic supply store. Hanging his helmet from a handlebar, he ran a hand through his hair as he headed inside. He swept through the store quickly, grabbing fistfuls of socks, athletic supporters and gym shorts.

"You outfitting the Olympic training team?" the clerk asked as he rang up the purchases.

"More or less." Russ pulled out his credit card, debating how best to con two proud teens into regarding the supplies as something other than a handout. "I've got a couple of buddies down at the Youth Center."

Russ didn't miss the disdain that flickered across the face of the college-age student. A lot of people had a similar reaction to the grungy gymnasium where the city had launched Youth Power, an afternoon program aimed at helping to keep high-risk kids from dropping out of school. The reaction wasn't so much over the building, as against the kids inside it—blacks, Cubans, Mexicans; poor, lagging behind in school; neglected if not abused. Teenagers who had to compete with drug pushers for territory on school grounds and parks.

They were kids like André and Howie, who were nursing bad blisters because they couldn't afford athletic socks. But not for much longer, if Russ had anything to do with it. He'd made himself that promise late last week, when he'd first spotted them limping off the court. Concerned, he'd followed them outside the building, where he'd insisted they stay off the court if they weren't going to wear socks.

André's defensiveness and Howie's shamefaced downward glance made Russ realize that the boys weren't playing sockless on purpose—they *didn't have* socks. And they certainly couldn't afford to buy them.

With painful clarity, Russ recalled his own humiliation in junior high, when he'd quit playing hoops because his grandmother had insisted on darning his worn-out socks with multicolored remnants of leftover yarn—

a humiliation no amount of wisecracking had been able to overcome.

It had been like that with the kids at the Youth Center from the very beginning; he understood where they were coming from—because he could remember all too well what it had been like for himself. Russ had volunteered for the center at the beginning of the school year, when WKIX had adopted the project as part of its annual community service. Although at first he'd simply considered it part of his duties as a 'KIX on-air personality, Russ had been immediately hooked by the kids. They were just like himself at that age—pretending to be tough to disguise their vulnerability.

André and Howie were his favorites.

His relationship with them had been cemented early in September, when Russ realized the two boys were coming to the center hungry. Whatever breakfast they'd had, and whatever meager lunch they'd taken from home couldn't have gone far. Without making a big deal about it, Russ had asked the two boys to run down Tennessee Street to the nearest burger stand with him, telling them how much he hated eating alone.

So, one of many rituals among the three had begun.

Russ found it difficult not to be concerned about how little the boys ate on days when he couldn't get to the center. But he knew better than to embarrass them by bringing it up—just as he should have known better than to make an issue of the blisters on their heels.

Right now, waiting for the clerk to run his credit card through the electronic cash register, Russ was still uncomfortable with how obtuse he'd been about the socks. Where were André and Howie supposed to get money for athletic socks? André had five brothers and sisters.

And Howie's mother—a single mother who was no doubt years younger than Russ—had a habit of leaving home for weeks at a time when the spirit moved her.

Russ was determined to find a way to persuade them to accept his purchases.

"Say, I know you." The clerk snapped his fingers as he waited for the register to compute the transaction. "You're the DJ from 'KIX. 'Russ for Rush Hour.'"

Russ smiled the picture-perfect smile he'd grown to hate, thanks to those billboards all over Florida's panhandle. "That's right. You listen to 'KIX?"

"Usually." He handed Russ the credit-card slip and a pen. "Except this morning. I was running the dial and heard this cool chick. She was a riot. I listened to the whole show before I remembered I hate that oldies junk."

Russ's smile didn't falter as he signed the slip and grabbed his purchases.

As he strapped the package onto the back of his black and silver bike, Russ calculated how long it would be before the next ratings came out. Not long—just about long enough for the effect of Jammin' J.T. to be evident. Could he muster the enthusiasm to gear up for the competition?

It wouldn't be the first time. Russ had been on top a long time, and plenty of other stations had brought in big names to bring him down. But no one had been good enough to touch his ratings. Yet one slip in the Arbitrons could be enough to make his reign precarious. Station managers like Tony Covington were loyal to only one thing: the ratings book.

So far, Russ had been lucky. He jammed his helmet on and impatiently kicked the bike's engine to life.

So far, he'd never been up against Jammin' J.T.

JILLIAN SIGHED WITH satisfaction as she signed off and turned the control room over to midmorning DJ Bruce Webb.

"Great job, J.T.," Bruce said as he leaned in close to adjust the height of the microphone boom. "You're going to be a tough act to follow every morning."

Easing away from the not-so-subtle physical contact, Jillian flashed the station's heartthrob a grateful smile as she cleared the control panel. "You can handle it—I hear the women eat you up."

"Maybe." His cocky smile belied the modest reply. Bruce's resonant voice lowered seductively. "Let me know if you need any help settling in."

"I'll file that thought away."

Slipping her feet back into the thigh-high suede boots she had shed halfway through the program, Jillian headed down the hall to stash her headset and check in with Jim Towers. She retouched her berry-colored lip gloss and grinned at herself in her pocket mirror, wondering if Towers would like the purple-and-teal lightning bolts of eye shadow she'd applied at the corners of her eyes this morning.

Thawing Jim Towers, she told herself as she opened the door to his office in response to his barked command, *may be a bigger challenge than building a new audience.*

Towers intended to play games—that much was instantly obvious. He lolled back in his swivel armchair and gave her a hard stare as she settled into the chair across from him. His crisp, contained mustache bracketed pursed lips. It was time for Towers to learn that Jillian Joyner didn't like games, she decided.

"Well?" She let her skirt hike up another inch as she crossed one knee over the other, then tossed her head so that her wine-red curls spilled over the back of her chair. "Did you like what you heard?"

"Whether I liked it or not isn't really the issue, is it? Will the listeners like you? That's the issue."

Jillian wanted to groan out loud, but kept her expression agreeably neutral. He apparently liked to act as pompous as he looked. "We won't know that for a while, will we? But you're the big man on campus and I'd like to hear what you think."

He studied her in silence for another long moment. Jillian recognized the technique and didn't let it get to her. She studied him just as attentively, until he began shifting in his chair. Even the toughest guys couldn't seem to handle it when a little ditz held her own. Jillian had learned early on what an advantage that gave her.

"The only thing you need to know right now is this," Towers finally said. "Russ Flynn is number one in the morning. Has been for a half-dozen years. Six months from now, I want the ratings to tell a different tale."

Russ Flynn. The morning man at WKIX, a country station that carried the adult market all day—thanks to Flynn. As the morning went, so went the rest of the day. That was a commonly held axiom in the radio-ratings wars waged all over the country. It was a high-stakes war, with millions of dollars in advertising riding on those quarterly ratings.

"Do you read me? I want you to take out Russ Flynn."

Flynn. She might've known. Billboards plastered with his grinning face lined the highways from the moment Jillian crossed the Georgia border into Florida's panhandle the week before. By the time she'd pulled the U-Haul trailer into the parking lot of her new condominium complex, she had been sick to death of his ear-to-ear grin.

"Russ Flynn doesn't worry me." She settled back in her chair and looked Towers square in the eye. "If you expect me to take Flynn out of the running, that's exactly what I'll do."

Her confidence seemed to irritate Towers.

"Flynn's been on top too long. I want his number-one spot for WFLA." He stood and tossed the latest Arbitrons in her lap. "You're only here because you had the Atlanta market sewn up. If you can't do the same in Tallahassee, you won't be here long. Got it?"

She took a deep breath, regretful for one moment that her past had caught up with her in Atlanta. "Got it. I'm in. Flynn's out."

THE ONLY SAVING GRACE *about a schedule that demands rising at 4:30 a.m.*, Jillian thought as she peeled off her suede boots and tossed them in the general direction of the closet, *is getting home in the middle of the afternoon.*

The bright sunshine pouring into her bedroom from the balcony overlooking the pool was very tempting. And Jillian planned to make the most of it, knowing that later in the spring and early summer, afternoon rainfall occurred almost daily.

Black textured stockings. Leather miniskirt. Cropped cotton sweater. One by one, they followed the suede boots into the corner of the room. Still clad in a rose silk teddy, she halted at the sight of the bold geometric comforter on the bed, which she'd haphazardly pulled up over the rumpled sheets when she left the house before dawn.

"Learn a little discipline, Miss Jillian." Her face shriveled into tight primness. She took a minute to straighten the comforter, hating herself even as she completed the action. "Much better, wouldn't you say, Miss Jillian?" she said aloud, mimicking that voice from her childhood that she so despised.

To this day, she hated a neat house; it reminded her of housekeepers and nannies and chauffeurs—people who'd been paid to replace mothers and fathers and sisters and brothers. Right now, she couldn't even recall the name of the prune-faced woman she had just imitated; she was simply one of many who had come and gone.

Jillian whisked around to face the mirror spanning the sliding doors of her walk-in closet. There in the mirror was Jammin' J.T.

"You're history for today, J.T.," she announced. "We're home now. Jillian lives."

After peeling off the teddy, she stepped into the bathroom and opened the cabinet door. The false eyelashes came off first, followed by the gaudy eye-shadow outlining her eyes. Then the berry-red lips were cleansed away. And after two minutes in the shower, the burgundy curls became a stream of light brown waves. Moussed-in color—the last vestige of Jammin' J.T.—washed down the drain.

Jillian slipped into a taupe maillot hanging on the back of the bathroom door, topping it with an oversize white oxford-cloth shirt. Then she pulled her hair to one side and braided it. With a quick glance in the mirror, she shoved the cabinet door shut.

"They'll never find you in there," she gloated to the bottles and jars that helped her create Jammin' J.T. The woman staring back at her from the mirror was plain, unassuming, maybe even mousy by some standards—certainly by Jammin' J.T.'s standards.

She was a woman no one would notice—much less recognize—on the street.

And that was *just* the way Jillian wanted it.

COVERED WITH SUNSCREEN, her eyes hidden behind tortoiseshell sunglasses, her face shaded by the wide brim of a straw hat, Jillian dozed in a lounge chair by the isolated pool. At this hour of the day, virtually everyone else in the singles complex was slaving away at whatever paid the bills. With a book at her side, Jillian relished the quiet and the solitude.

A sudden splash, accompanied by a few spatters of cool water against her calves, made her reluctantly open her eyes. She watched a pair of well-muscled tanned shoulders and strong arms thrashing through the water. Taut buttocks clad in red swimming trunks broke the surface.

A Florida sun god. Self-conscious about her curiosity, Jillian glanced around the pool. There was no one else in sight. And the swimmer had placed his belongings on a lounge chair at the far end of the pool. Good. Jillian's eyelids drifted shut again. Maybe she could slip back into the daydream—her favorite fantasy, the one she'd been dreaming ever since the day of her tenth birthday, when on a celebration ride on the carnival Ferris wheel, it had stalled with her stuck alone in the swaying wooden seat at the very top. Surprisingly, instead of being frightened, she'd been exhilarated. Far below, she could barely see her mother in the mass of people. And, in the half hour the Ferris wheel was stalled, Jillian—for the first time in her life—begun to imagine she was someone else.

Now, she attempted to resurrect that familiar fantasy. Alone on the Ferris wheel, she pictured herself high above the lights and noise of a carnival. But it wasn't high enough to suit her. She kept urging the Ferris-wheel operator to take the ride higher—so high that no one on the ground could reach her; so high she no longer had to be Jillian Tate Joyner. She could simply drift, losing herself in the peaceful solitude.

But before the fantasy could take shape, she was disturbed by the sound of splashing. Instantly, she was aware that someone was looking at her.

"Hope I didn't splash you when I dived in."

The voice was warm, deep, and just a tad mischievous. Jillian frowned as she looked up, ready to be cool and dismissive.

The eyes she looked into were warm and startling blue in color. A clear, bright, sky blue. The blue of the sky that encircled her on her imaginary Ferris wheel. An enticing blue that was anything but tranquil.

The eyes were also familiar. In fact, the entire face was familiar. As it should be. After all, it had stared at her from billboard after billboard as she'd driven along the Florida highway. Immediately, her feeling of contentment was replaced with panic.

Russ Flynn.

Suddenly her new hideaway seemed like no hideaway after all.

2

HER NUMBER-ONE RIVAL, right here in her own backyard. Would he connect Jillian Joyner and Jammin' J.T.? If not now, later? And what would happen when he did penetrate her disguise? Would her private life become a battle ground in the ratings war?

Russ Flynn smiled at her while water dripped off his strong nose and thick lashes. His lazy, appraising grin made her skin prickle.

Apprehension, she told herself. And something else...

Making an effort to regain her composure, Jillian tapped at her sunglasses, making sure they were still in place. The brim of her hat, pulled low over her forehead, brushed her knuckles.

Okay, kiddo. Let's see if you can really act. Or is all that phony, too?

"I...I'm sorry. Did you say something?" Her voice wouldn't give her away. He couldn't recognize it yet. She'd only been in town one day. *Be cool. This is just a coincidence.*

"No, *I'm* sorry." He rested his arms on the side of the pool, bringing his sleek, olive-toned shoulders directly into view. "I thought maybe I'd splashed you, but I bet I've just managed to wake you instead."

"That's all right." Her head dropped back against the lounge chair again and she closed her eyes. She was surprised to find herself a bit breathless. *Why doesn't he swim away?*

"I'm Russ Flynn. I live in C-18."

Water splashed again as he hoisted himself up to sit on the side of the pool. Jillian lifted one eyelid just enough to view him. And wished she hadn't. He was tanned and sleek all over—hard calves and well-toned thighs, slim hips beneath the water-drenched swimsuit, a belly hard and flat and bisected by a downward swirl of wet curls, a muscular chest. How would it feel to . . .?

She closed her eyes. *Why the hell doesn't he go away?*

"And you're Greta Garbo. You 'yust vant to be left alone.' Right?"

Those words, spoken in his deep, soft voice, resurrected her fears. And a restless stirring. Her mouth went dry. She leveled her dark glasses on him and found his straightforward blue gaze disconcerting.

"That's right."

Before she could sink back in her chair, he unfolded his long, dripping frame and stood towering over her.

"I can accept that." His relaxed expression signaled that her abruptness hadn't miffed him. "But first, I have to know one thing. Are you a new but permanent fixture here at Wendover Court? Or just a ship passing in the night? Only a visitor to my fair city?"

When she stared at him, his grin widened until it was almost as broad as the caricatures on the billboards. His smile was certainly seductive. Too damn enticing for her peace of mind. Russ Flynn was definitely dangerous.

"I know." He nodded, matching her serious expression with one of his own. "On the face of it, that seems to be none of my business. But look at it from my standpoint. I *need* to know. I mean, as I sit across the pool, entertaining fantasies of falling madly in lust with you, should I also entertain just a little bit of hope that one day you'll slip that tiny foot into the glass slipper? Let me save you from the poison apple? Kiss me and turn me into a prince? Or should I resign myself to this one shining moment—never to see you again once you've packed yourself off for the return trip to Waukegan, Illinois. Or wherever."

Definitely a DJ. Only a DJ could come up with so much blarney on such short notice. It reflects years of training.

"Are you always so full of . . . malarkey?"

He laughed—a low, intimate rumble. She felt herself melting.

Russ Flynn, she reminded herself. *This is Russ Flynn. Not a person you can afford to get chummy with.*

"Not always. If you won't laugh, I'll tell you a secret."

She made no promises; she was too taken by his unexpected openness. If this was an act, it was a good one.

"Sometimes it's all I can do to work up the nerve to talk to women. Some women, anyway." He grinned again, a tentative smile that was ten times more endearing than the bold smile he'd started with. "The . . . What did you call it? Malarkey? Makes it easier. So you could say I'm mostly full of it—but not always."

She didn't want to know any more. She didn't want to know why some women intimidated him. Or why that brought out the malarkey in him. She definitely didn't want to know.

"And I just happen to bring out the malarkey in you?" Now, why did she say that? Why didn't she simply pick up her book and wait for him to sink back into the water?

He squatted, lowering one knee to the tile, which brought him to eye level with her. His gaze searched her face. She almost panicked, then reassured herself that both her hat and sunglasses were securely in place.

"That's right." She flinched when he reached over and tapped the cover of her book. "Because when I noticed you were reading the same book I'm reading, I felt sure it was fate. How often is somebody else at the pool reading the history of vaudeville?"

His tone was serious. If there was a trace of mockery in his words, she couldn't find it. "And looking fate in the eye—that can be intimidating."

She was only momentarily sidetracked by the sincerity in his face. The book. *Omigosh, the book.* She looked down at the book she had let flop open across her midriff, and suppressed the urge to cover it with her hands. "You're kidding?"

"No. Doesn't that sort of give you a free-fall right about here?" He punched his midsection. Jillian forced herself not to follow his gesture.

"I mean the book. You're kidding about the book. Right?"

He pointed to the oversize blue book he'd left with his striped towel. "No. For the moment, at least, I'm perfectly serious." He held up a finger. "I'm assuming that doesn't automatically sufficiently endear me to you. Still, can I convince you to give up a nap in the sunshine? Have pity on me. Do you live here? Will I see you again? Do you have a name? Do you turn into a pumpkin at midnight?"

In her time, Jillian had observed many such lustful gazes—all of them directed at J.T.; none of them directed at plain-Jane Jillian. J.T. knew how to handle them. Jillian, however, was flustered and fascinated and almost flattered enough to forget why she shouldn't be interested. Or even friendly.

But ignoring knees that had turned to rubber wasn't easy. And, really, he was entirely too charming for her to act like a total jerk—so charming she could almost buy his vulnerability.

"I do live here," she admitted briskly. "My name is Jillian." She hesitated. "Joyner. Jillian Joyner. But I don't wear glass slippers. And I *do* want to be left alone."

"And not just today." It wasn't a question.

"And not just today."

"Then I will worship from afar." With an unperturbed smile, he turned to leave, pausing a few steps away. "But if you find you're having poison-apple problems . . ."

"I'll check the yellow pages."

"Russ Flynn. C-18. In case you forgot."

"I didn't forget."

SHE COULDN'T FORGET, she discovered as she set her VCR to tape the late news so she could watch it before heading to the station before sunup the next morning. She couldn't get the blasted man out of her head.

It wasn't so much Russ Flynn—although she had been unpleasantly surprised by how appealing he was. It was what his unexpected intrusion on her life represented: more upheaval—and worse, exposure.

She went through her bedtime routine of choosing—from the J.T. side of her closet—the clothes she would put on at four-thirty the next morning. As she browsed through the recently unpacked clothes, she recalled the conversation that had taken place in Atlanta just weeks before, when she was folding those same clothes and packing them in boxes.

Anne Marie, her closest friend in Atlanta, had been outraged that Jillian would quit her job and leave town simply because a reporter from the *Atlanta Constitution* had discovered Jammin' J.T.'s identity. Anne Marie thought Jillian was exaggerating when she tried to describe the publicity and attention that would follow such a disclosure.

And in the end, Anne Marie had berated her, asking if Tallahassee would be any different.

Good question, Jillian thought as she yanked a dress out of the closet. Here in Tallahassee, where the media glare was dimmer and celebrity not such a major issue, she had hoped that keeping her past under wraps wouldn't be as tough.

But if Russ Flynn—the nemesis she was out to conquer, the star she was here to outshine—lived in her own backyard, how long would it be before the secret was out?

She was tempted to call Anne Marie and moan in her friend's sympathetic ear. But she didn't have to. She could hear Anne Marie's goading drawl even without the long-distance hookup. "How long's it going to be before you run again, Jillie?"

As Jillian slipped between the sheets and reached over to turn out the brass lamp on her bedside table, a small, framed snapshot caught her eye. Standing on the massive, snow-covered stone steps of an old courthouse in Connecticut, a woman was laughing heartily, her red hair dazzling in the sunshine. Huddled deeply against the woman's sable coat was a solemn, wide-eyed child.

Jillian remembered the exact words Audrey Tate was whispering through her unwavering smile as dozens of photographers snapped the same photo. "I want you to call him Daddy, sweetheart. As soon as they finish this photo, I want you to tell all the reporters how glad you are to have a new daddy. Okay?"

Twenty years later, Jillian could still remember how she had stiffened, trying to pull away from her determined mother. "No. I already have a daddy. I don't need a new daddy."

"Of course you do, lovey. Now, be sweet and do what Mommy tells you."

Jillian had looked through the crowd, wondering if her real father—the one the judge had just said was no longer married to her mother—would be there. Wondering if he might tug on her ear and pull her into his lap and tell her one of his funny stories.

He hadn't been there, of course. There was no ear tugging, and no laps and no stories. Only reporters and photographers and the woman in the sable coat.

So Jillian had looked up into her mother's dramatic green eyes, which were cold with insistence, and at her lips, which were frozen into the smile the camera adored, and she had spoken the words her mother wanted to hear. Audrey Tate didn't often get angry. But Jillian had known, even at the age of eight, that one sure way to infuriate Audrey was to breach her authority when reporters were around.

"They'll crucify you, Jillie," her mother had told her that morning, the way she'd told her many times before and after. "If they think they can draw blood, they'll nail you every time. Remember that, Jillie."

Jillian had remembered that and told everyone gathered for the occasion how glad she was to have a new daddy.

The memories were all wrapped up with the sharp Connecticut cold, the crunch of tires grinding over ice, the feel of the sable against her cheek. And the sable hadn't felt warm at all. It had been cool. As cool as the three-karat rock the legendary Audrey Tate had acquired that day upon announcing that she'd celebrated her divorce with a surprise wedding to one of Hollywood's most famous producers.

Jillian didn't even know why she kept the photo, except that it was one of the few that had never been published. Almost every other photograph of her childhood had been reprinted in magazines, newspapers, tabloids. So she'd always tried to separate the picture from her memories of that day, tried to pretend it wasn't just another one of those days she wanted to forget.

It didn't always work.

Disgusted to think that her mother still had her on the run at the age of twenty-eight, Jillian turned the photo facedown before she turned out the light.

J.T. WAS PROPERLY DECKED out for a deadly serious marketing-strategy meeting—spiked hair verging on the color of Florida oranges; enormous gold earrings in the shape of a lion's head dangling almost to her shoulders; eye makeup in smoldering gold tones that gave her the look of a predatory cat; and a poured-to-fit leopard-print knit dress with a high neck and correspondingly high hemline.

Her shoes, however, were demure black pumps—with five-inch heels.

She sat quietly across from the afternoon DJ, who wore a neon-bright tie shaped like a fish. She hoped he felt shown up in his feeble attempt to be outrageous—no one out-outrageoused Jammin' J.T.

This morning, however, that fact brought little satisfaction. What she really wanted to be this morning was Jillian. A Jillian who didn't have to worry about who might recognize her at the pool. A Jillian who could have responded to Russ's flirtation without guilt or fear. The quiet, undramatic, uncomplicated Jillian she had been repressing since childhood.

But there was no time for that Jillian. It was time for J.T. to worry about audience share and market saturation.

"...Exactly what J.T. is doing here." Jim Towers's imperious words caught her attention. "Nobody's invincible—not even Flynn. And J.T.'s just the one to drive that lesson home."

Her heart pounded at the mention of his name. To everyone else around the table, Russ Flynn was numbers in a rating book and a caricature grinning down from a billboard. To Jillian, he was the man who'd set her pulse racing the previous afternoon. Solely because of the threat he posed, naturally.

For a moment, she was distracted by the image of Russ Flynn's taut body looming over hers.

"A force to be reckoned with for more than five years." Rosa Miguel, the station's marketing director was talking. "He's a Tallahassee native. He's genuine. He's active in the community. And he's got brains."

Rosa directed her dark, piercing eyes at Jillian. Her inference was crystal clear—*Does this woman whose dress fits like a second skin have a brain in her head?* Jillian smiled blandly, knowing it was a natural response to J.T. from someone who wore dress-for-success suits and neatly coiffed hair.

"He's got brains," Jillian conceded, forcing herself to concentrate only on the numbers in the rating books when she thought of Russ Flynn. "But he's also riding the crest of a country-music craze that's turning into foam on the beach. Tallahassee's population is aging—and that over-thirty crowd goes for the oldies in a big way. And the college-age segment of the market certainly isn't hot for country.

"Even Russ Flynn isn't good enough to survive that."

The struggle to say his name without conjuring unwelcome images was worth it when Rosa's skeptical expression disappeared. Jillian smiled again—the tangerine Betty Boop smile that brought out her dimple. Rosa smiled back, abandoning for the moment her professional cool. Then Jillian intuited that Rosa's formality was her means of protection against little Napoleons like Jim Towers.

Rosa Miguel's smooth-as-glass surface was as much an act as Jillian's own daily charade as J.T. Jillian liked it. She liked Rosa. It was just a shame she couldn't do anything about it. Getting tight with the publicity pusher—definitely not smart.

"J.T.'s right," Jim Towers said. "Now's the time to let the air out of Flynn's tires. I'm tired of the way he leaves us in the slow lane every time the ratings come out. We're going to grind him into scrap metal, boys and girls."

A challenging look in Jillian's corner accompanied his last words.

"J.T.'s first two shows were strong," the afternoon announcer conceded. "But Flynn's so entrenched in Tallahassee. Isn't J.T.'s newness going to work against her?"

"Not if we get her out in the community while her novelty is still a drawing card," Towers replied. "Jammin' J.T.'s going to hit the road running."

"Will public appearances be enough?" Rosa asked.

"It had better be. If we don't kill Flynn's domination, we're going to see a lot of other changes around here." At Towers's words, all eyes once again shifted in Jillian's direction. Now it wasn't just her job on the line, but theirs, too. Jillian wondered if it was too early to decide she hated her new boss. "But with the calendar of public appearances we've got lined up for J.T. in the next three months, the public can't help but react."

Rosa and Jillian locked gazes again. This time, as Towers's last words sank in, there was a touch of real humor in Rosa's expression.

"No doubt about that. They'll most certainly react once they see her." Rosa's gold pen tapped on her clipboard as she scrutinized Jillian's appearance. "So, curiosity gets them to tune in? Then what?"

"Then I hook them," Jillian announced with the vacuous smile she knew was completely at odds with the confidence in her voice. The marketing director's half smile and the spark in her dark eyes indicated that she appreciated the contrast. Only another astute woman who played the same game successfully would realize Jillian's image was one she cultivated to make herself less threatening.

"You're that confident?" Rosa asked.

"I'm that good."

Rosa laughed—the laugh of someone who liked what she'd heard. Others around the table joined her. But the others, Jillian could tell, weren't quite sure of the joke.

"She is that good," the ad manager spoke up. "We've already had calls from a couple of sponsors wanting to double up on their exposure during morning drive-time."

"She'd better be that good."

Jillian was growing weary of having Towers talk over her head, as if she were a racehorse hired to perform but not to participate in the decision-making.

"I'll do my part, Towers." She matched his imperious tone. "Now you do yours. How much money is the station going to put into promoting me?"

"Plenty." Towers named a figure that momentarily stunned everyone in the room, including Rosa. "Believe me, if we can bury Flynn, it'll be worth twice that in ad revenues in the last quarter of this year."

"Then tell me what kind of public exposure you've got in mind." Rosa's tone matched the hard, humorless edge in Towers's voice. "If we're going to stick it to Russ Flynn, we've got work to do."

Jillian resisted the urge to shift uncomfortably in her seat as Towers passed around an itinerary of public appearances for J.T. She reflected that it would have been a lot easier to plot the demise of a competitor's career before she knew that competitor firsthand. *But*, she warned herself, *that's what you were hired to do, and that's what you'll do.*

"A newspaper interview shouldn't be tough to arrange," Rosa replied, making a note on her clipboard. "And maybe we can put together a—"

"I don't do interviews."

Jim Towers mobilized for battle while the others shifted away from him, wanting to avoid the cross fire.

Rosa looked puzzled and faintly amused. "No interviews?"

"None." Jillian lifted her chin up a notch. "Photos are fine. I'll answer questions for anybody when I'm making an appearance. But no in-depth interviews."

"Why the hell not?" Towers demanded, his sandy mustache twitching as if he were sniffing the air in anticipation of bloodshed.

Jillian smiled sweetly. "Because it's nobody's business what I sleep in or what kind of dog I had when I was growing up. I won't have some turkey spend an hour asking me inane questions so he can write about my life as if he's known me since kindergarten." She turned back to Rosa. "No interviews."

"You'll do interviews if—"

Towers's ultimatum was cut off by Rosa's calm voice. "Actually, Towers, that has good possibilities. J.T.'s face will be everywhere. Her voice will be everywhere. But nobody will really know anything about her. There'll be an element of…mystery…about her. Let's work on that, Towers. I think we can use it."

Towers looked inclined to disagree on principle. "I don't know…."

"It'll work," Rosa countered. "I'd bet my boat on it. You want to talk curiosity? I'll give you curiosity. We'll make WFLA's Tallahassee Lassie a real mystery lady."

THE NEXT AFTERNOON, as Russ followed Jillian out to the pool, he kept reassuring himself that he was intrigued simply because she was nothing like the luscious but plastic sophisticates who threw themselves in the paths of DJs—luscious sophisticates he'd had trouble turning away from at first, but who now left him cold.

Jillian was unabashedly real and unapologetically prickly—which made ordinary conversation a challenge. Not at all concerned with graciousness or feminine wiles, she jumped back at him with a pointedly abrasive retort every time he opened his mouth.

Far from Miss-America stunning, she was just the kind of woman he'd fantasized about for years, while doing the rounds with the boring beauties. Recently he'd practically sworn off women because he hadn't met one who had a clue who he really was. Or who *they* really were, for that matter. The meager rewards of casual sex hadn't seemed worth the risk anymore.

But Jillian . . . She was the stuff of fantasies—*his* kind of fantasies, at least. The kind of woman who was too smart for him to snow with one of his weak-kneed lines. Who could stand up to him and give back as good as she got. Who would realize there was more to Russ Flynn than snappy patter from six to ten. Maybe, just maybe, a woman who wouldn't expect him to be Mr. Perfection, either.

Exteriors aside, this was one hell of an appealing woman.

He decided to forgo the lounge chair on the opposite side of the pool in favor of the one next to Jillian, then had second thoughts. Was he really up to this? After all, his basic training might not have prepared him for a real, complex, complicated woman. A woman like this would expect him to have the depth to match hers. Russ swallowed hard as he drew close.

"Do you ever get wet?" He dropped into the chair, wondering why her sedate maillot was more enticing than a string bikini. "Or are you just here for the scenery?"

"I'm a sun worshipper." As she spoke, she pulled the brim of her hat lower over her face. "Conversation disturbs the rays. Makes them wavy. Then I tan unevenly. You wouldn't want that on your conscience, would you?"

"I could live with it." He hadn't noticed it the day before, but he suddenly realized that her hair was pulled back in a thick, loose braid that trailed down her back— way down her back. He considered the possibilities of loosening the braid, of letting the long, auburn strands float, trailing over her body—trailing over his body.... He refocused on the tense-looking woman beside him. "Sun worshipper, huh? Naw, I don't buy it. You're using number thirty-two sunscreen. Your book shades the tops of your thighs—no self-respecting sun worshiper would let that happen. And I'll bet—" he leaned closer and lowered his voice"—I'll bet if I peeked just under the edge of that swimsuit, you've barely got a tan line."

He would have sworn that her pulse leaped at the base of her throat. Or perhaps it was the leap of his own pulse.

"Mr. Flynn, is it inconceivable to you that being entertained by your boyish charm isn't high on my to-do list for the day?"

"Now, *that* I can believe." He whipped the towel from around his neck and draped it smoothly over the back of a lounge chair before settling into it. He'd been right: he wasn't ready for this. He plowed ahead anyway. "Boyish charm gets old in a hurry, doesn't it? Kind of like gushy women."

She lifted the rim of her hat to peer at him in silence. Completely without intending to, he smiled at her.

"You can hardly blame me if you came along just when I was getting tired of gushy women."

She pursed her lips. He would have bet his last pay raise that she did it to stifle a smile.

"If it will help to discourage you, I could try gushing."

"I don't think you're going to pull off a phony act very convincingly."

"Such an astute judge of character."

There she went again—giving him the impression that there were layers to this conversation he couldn't begin to fathom. The worst of it was, he liked the unsettled feeling it gave him—as if he could lose his footing at any minute. It was the same sensation he got on a dirt bike when he managed to hold it on the path in spite of rocks and gravel and ruts.

"And not easily discouraged, either. Anybody who knows me will tell you that." He willed his muscles to relax. "Kind of like a puppy. One scratch behind the ears and I'm your friend for life. That's me."

"Mr. Flynn..."

"Russ. You have to call me Russ. I'm over thirty now—just by two years, but over, nonetheless—and I get nervous when people call me Mr. Flynn." Why, he wondered, was he trying so desperately to impress her? And why, instead, was he managing to sound so junior-high-school dumb? "My father was mostly bald, you see, and when people call me Mr. Flynn I start wondering if it's started coming out already."

"Russ, I haven't scratched you behind the ears yet," she said crisply. "So, we aren't friends for life. Got it?"

"It is, isn't it?"

"What?" She slammed her book shut and faced him.

"The hair. It's getting thin, isn't it?" Patting the crown of his head in exploration, he struggled for the most dismayed look he could find. It worked. She laughed. He felt foolishly pleased with himself. "Aha! A laugh is as good as a scratch behind the ears. You've sealed it now. Friends for life."

He sat back in the chair, closed his eyes and folded his arms in contentment.

"What is it with you, Russ?" A hint of reluctant humor laced her voice. "You're lonely, right? The personal ads haven't worked. Your mother rejected you as a child. Or maybe you just have a fetish for women under five-one."

"I knew it. You do have a sense of humor. Anyone reading the history of vaudeville has to have a sense of humor. That's what I told myself when I saw you sitting out here yesterday, and I was absolutely right."

"I do *not* have a sense of humor."

Then, as if reacting to some inside joke, she laughed out loud again. He resisted the impulse to reach over and take off her sunglasses so he could see her eyes when she laughed. But as he watched her quickly bring her laughter under control, his former uneasiness gripped him.

This woman was too complicated. Not the kind of one-dimensional playgirl who never minded if all their conversations were superficial and their passion sort-term. His strong attraction to her wit and intelligence was accompanied by another new unsettling emotion: fear? Maybe a woman like this, a woman whose attractions went much deeper than the surface, wouldn't find much below his surface to attract her. Maybe he'd have been smarter, after all, to go for the superficial infatuation. He had a momentary impulse to flee.

Then he caught the twist of her wrist—her pale, fragile, graceful wrist—as she tried to pull her swimsuit lower on her thighs—her creamy white thighs—without him noticing. Maybe he would stay long enough to look her in the eye. Just once. "If you've got no sense of humor, what's so funny?"

"Nothing."

The sharpness of her clipped reply silenced him. She opened her book again. Now, he told himself, he really should leave. It wasn't as if he was mesmerized by her. Actually, she was kind of mousy.

Except for her hair. He wondered, how would her hair look loose against those lush breasts she was trying so desperately to hide with her sensible swimsuit.

He sighed. *What the hell is happening to me?* "Where do you work, that you're off in the middle of the afternoon?"

She stared straight into her book. "Perhaps I'm independently wealthy."

"Sure, I get it. Tallahassee, mecca for millionaires." He almost grinned. If she really hated him, she'd leave, wouldn't she? She wouldn't sit here swapping barbs. Would she? "You're not from Florida, are you?"

She opened her mouth to speak, closed it, then started over. "New England."

"Mmm, that explains everything. The stereotypical recalcitrant New Englander. Tell you what, I'll make this easier on you. I'll go first."

"Russ—"

"Age thirty-two. Born in Santiago, Florida, which sounds exotic but isn't. Farmers. Feed store. Dirt-poor and not much smarter. Barely made it through high school. Too much else to do." Russ realized that, irrationally, his heart was racing. When was the last time he'd told a woman this kind of stuff? If he ever had at all.

"I liked girls, but I liked dirt bikes more. But life led me in other directions. Like, to the barn. Spent more time milking cows than anything else." Abruptly, he switched into a mocking version of the deep, modulated voice of radio-and-TV announcers. "And my first stint as Captain Big Voice." He returned his voice to its normal timbre. "Radio. My high-school sweetheart and still the love of my life. Weekends and afternoons, that's all I wanted to do. No college. Too busy. Never married, although there was that one close call." The rush of words stopped. He sounded shallow, even to himself. This was all wasted effort. He drew a deep breath and dropped the edge of his towel, which he'd begun to unravel. "Now it's your turn."

He waited. Patiently. Well, perhaps impatiently. "Excuse me, miss. I believe it's your turn."

She stared at him intently from under the brim of her hat. "Age forty-nine. Born in Salem, on the site of a witch-burning. Degrees from Harvard, Yale and—"

"Hold on." With one swift movement he reached over and slipped her sunglasses off her nose, revealing her intense green eyes. "There. That's better. You know, you're marvelously well-preserved for forty-nine. Now, after Yale?"

For a moment he assumed she wasn't going to speak again. She simply stared at him, her eyes wide with surprise. Her hand fluttered upward and he had the impression that she wanted to cover her face.

"After Yale?" Her voice was almost timid, then she seemed to force herself to recover. "Ax murder, 1989."

She was shy. That was it. He should have realized it. She was shy and his anxiety was making him pursue her before he lost his nerve. He made up his mind to take it slower, not scare her off. "Ax murder? Fascinating. And the motive?"

She reached over and took the glasses from him. "Temporary insanity. I was trying to sunbathe. You know how it is. All you ask is a little peace and quiet."

Shoving her sunglasses on, she closed her book once again and shrugged into the oxford-cloth shirt draped over the arm of her chair. Then she leaned so close their noses almost met and started speaking in a menacing voice that sounded like the mad killer in a 1940s radio drama.

"Then some gregarious pain in the caboose came along and interrupted. I lost control. Not a court in the land would have convicted me."

She stood, the mad-killer gleam in her eyes gone, replaced by a benign smile. He might be in love. He wondered if she realized what a gift she had for humor. Yes, this could be love. She turned and started to walk away.

"You never did tell me where you work," he called after her.

"Didn't I?"

"No," he said, curious whether her hips were swaying that much solely for his benefit. It seemed unlikely, but it was a nice daydream. "You didn't."

"Isn't that odd?" With a flip of her hand, she signaled her goodbye and walked down the pathway to her building.

Disgruntled in spite of himself, Russ picked up the morning paper he'd brought with him to the pool—and found himself smiling at the idea of sharp-tongued Jillian Joyner wandering through one of the hoity-toity charity balls and political bashes that had once made up ninety percent of the social life he hated.

Nope, Jillian Joyner wouldn't like one of those parties any better than he did.

He could, however, see her living out the fantasy that had kept him sane every time he'd had to endure a bash like that—the one in which he roared through the door on his motorcycle, grabbed a glass of champagne from the tray of a stunned server, blew a kiss to the hostess, revved his bike's engine to an ear-stunning level and roared out through the patio.

Yep, that's just the kind of entrance and exit that would suit Jillian Joyner. And maybe it was just as well he'd been toying with the idea of making some drastic changes in his life lately.

3

JILLIAN HAD ARGUED with Rosa Miguel for three-quarters of an hour. And still Rosa wouldn't budge.

Jammin' J.T. was going on the air. With Russ Flynn.

"Are you sure about this?" Jillian tried one more time as they waited for the Florida State University campus station to begin its telephone interview with the two competitors.

"Trust me. It's brilliant." Rosa's smile was triumphant. She settled comfortably into a chair to listen to the publicity stunt that had left Jillian sleepless all night. "This is your chance to steal some of Flynn's faithfuls. They'll all be listening for him, but when they hear the Tallahassee Lassie . . ."

"I know. They'll be hooked."

Rosa winked and raised her left thumb, drawing Jillian's attention to the modest diamond solitaire on her ring finger. "And Towers thinks you're an airhead. I told him you'd catch on quick."

Jillian grinned at Rosa in spite of herself. "Towers thinks I'm a headache. That's what Towers thinks."

Smart retorts were easy now. But Jillian wondered if she would be able to keep her voice under control once the three-station telephone hookup was under way. What would she say to Russ? And what if he recognized her voice?

"You're right." Rosa crossed her legs and smoothed her linen skirt carefully over her knees, then looked up with a sly smile. "You *are* a headache. An expensive headache."

Jillian was growing comfortable with that smile—much more comfortable than she was with the more formal Rosa Miguel who roamed the halls at the station.

"So, what's with the rock?" She pointed to the ring. Rosa had been J.T.'s shadow since their marketing strategy meeting. She knew about Rosa's grandparents, who had refused to learn English after coming to Florida from Guatemala forty-one years earlier. She knew about her boat, which represented Rosa's statement to the world and her family that she had made it. She knew about Rosa's thirty-six carefully-labeled shoe boxes and the extra linen suit and silk blouse she kept in the trunk of her silver BMW convertible, "just in case." But she didn't know anything about a man in Rosa's life. "You've told me about your golf handicap, but not your fiancé."

Rosa looked down at the diamond. "I have the perfect fiancé. Quiet, undemanding, never fights with my family."

"How exciting. I can tell your heart really pitter-patters over that."

The sly grin was back. "He's everything I want in a man."

"Give, Miguel. I want to know more about Mr. Perfect."

"I bought it myself."

"You what?"

"I bought it myself." Rosa shrugged, looking almost sheepish. "It comes in handy sometimes, when you work with men all day."

Jillian was astonished. She had always figured she was the only woman in the business who didn't want to take advantage of the fact that there were so many eligible men in their field. "You mean you *want* to keep the men away?"

"Why does that surprise you? So do you."

Fairness dictated that, if she could peg Rosa so easily, it followed that Rosa could also read her well. But it always surprised Jillian, anyway. "Well, I . . . It's not . . ."

"Not the same? Maybe not. Maybe I don't get involved to make sure I'm always taken seriously. What's your excuse?"

The tactic worked, Jillian realized. Everyone respected Rosa. And no one else seemed to recognize the dual personality Jillian had spotted almost immediately—the sharp-witted Rosa Miguel who surfaced when they were together was nothing like the deadly serious "suit" who sat in on WFLA strategy meetings and held her own with Jim Towers.

"My excuse?" Jillian looked down at today's flirty little dress. "The same, I guess. I just want them to take me seriously."

Rosa laughed. "That's okay, mystery lady. I'll figure you out before it's over."

She had tried, Jillian had to give her that much. At first, Rosa had invited her to play tennis on those rare afternoons when J.T. had no appearances. When that failed, she had suggested they stop for dinner after a couple of J.T.'s remotes. So far, Jillian had always made an excuse. But in spite of herself, she was being drawn into a wary friendship with the woman whose job it was to thrust her into the limelight—just what Jillian dreaded most. Yet Rosa's mischievousness made her hard to resist.

It was tough to keep in mind, given the circumstances, that Rosa wasn't prime pal material. It might have been easier if she could just convince herself that she didn't like Rosa Miguel.

Jillian jumped as her headset popped. The lines were open. The throaty voice of the young female announcer for the campus station signaled Jillian that they were about to go on the air.

"I'm ready." *In a pig's eye.*

"Same here."

Russ. His voice brushed intimately against her ears. Her heart pounded. Was it too late to back out of this?

Rosa's chair blocked the door of the cramped studio.

"Listen up, boys and girls," the young woman was saying. "This is Andi Vogel on WFSU and our interview this afternoon is a real treat. In the next few weeks, Tallahassee is going to mobilize for battle. We'll all be choosing sides. And for a preview of the skirmishes to come, we're going to talk this afternoon with the two people on the front lines of that battle—longtime WKIX morning man Russ Flynn and the new Tallahassee Lassie, WFLA's Jammin' J.T."

In a few concise sentences, Andi filled her audience in on the background of her two guests, then opened with a question.

"The first thing I want to know is, have you two met yet?"

Jillian's head jerked up so fast she almost lost her headset. "No. No, we haven't."

"But I'd like to." Russ's voice over her headset was all friendly seduction. She could imagine his eyes—those piercing blue eyes that didn't know how to look any way but inviting. "How about breakfast tomorrow, J.T.?"

Jillian stared at the control panel in front of her, unable to force a single word out of her mouth.

"Lighten up, lady!" Rosa hissed.

"Sorry, Russ," she said numbly, trying to call up the professionalism that had seemed to abandon her at the sound of his voice. This wasn't going to work! "I believe I've got a prior engagement first thing in the morning."

Andi laughed. "J.T., I'm going to cut right to the chase. Word on the street is that you're a hired gun. Brought in to gun down 'Russ for Rush Hour.' Is that true?"

Funny. She had to be funny.

"Well, I wouldn't say I'm a hired gun, exactly." What was Russ thinking? Did she sound familiar to him? "But we have set up a 'KIX billboard for target practice in the control room. And my aim's getting a lot better."

"That explains those headaches I've been getting," Russ countered. She could hear the wry grin in his voice. "They start right between the eyes."

"Does that mean you're worried?" Andi asked.

Jillian heard his split second of hesitation. She felt a moment of thrill that came from knowing she had the competition's attention.

Then she remembered who the competition was.

"Worried? I wouldn't say I'm worried. J.T. hasn't had time to put down any roots in the Panhandle yet. She's probably still trying to figure out where Tallahassee's beach is."

Jillian bristled at the implication she didn't know her way around the town that had no beach. The sparring had to start sometime, she reminded herself. The campus station hadn't brought them together in hopes they would stroke each other.

"I'll let you work on figuring that out, Flynn. Here's a clue: Ponder the word *landlocked*." She forced a droll lightness into her voice. "I'm a lot more concerned with figuring out what's going on at the capitol."

"Ha! You're following the sex-crime trial, right?"

"We don't need sex-crime trials to spice up the Wake-Up Call, Russ. Does that kind of thing work for you?"

"You're not following the sex-crime trial? The model and the politician? Hot stuff."

"No, thanks. I read the news, not the gossip."

"You don't think a politician up to his Jockey shorts in a sex scandal is news?"

Jillian wondered if the politician had children—and hoped not. "I don't get my kicks that way. And I honestly don't believe that anybody's sex habits are big news."

"Why not? Don't his constituents deserve to know what—"

"Nobody needs to know what's going on in somebody else's bedroom." From the corner of her eye, Jillian saw Rosa giving her a thumbs-up signal.

"Does that mean you're uptight about sex, J.T.?" His voice was a silky caress. Jillian felt it rippling along her nerve endings.

"Does that mean you're preoccupied with sex, Russ?" She didn't feel nearly as prim and proper as she sounded.

So they argued. For about half an hour, while Andi kept her mouth shut and the phone lines open, they sniped and pricked. Jillian's long nails had gouged deep ridges in her palms by the time Andi spoke again.

"Listen, you two, that's all the time we've got today. But I'd love to set up another free-for-all sometime soon."

"I'd love that," Jillian purred, although her stomach churned.

"See you around, J.T." The intimate sound of Russ's sign-off set Jillian to worrying. Did he know something, after all?

Disconnecting herself from the equipment, Jillian moved slowly and deliberately to give herself time to stop shaking.

"Wow!" Rosa was on her feet. "You two really sizzled, J.T. Have you ever thought about teaming up with somebody like Flynn?"

"Bite your tongue."

"Not that you need a partner to prop you up. It's just... Something really clicked when you two started taking shots at each other. I wonder if Towers has ever thought about a male-female team?"

Jillian grimaced at the mention of the station manager's name. "I thought we'd agreed not to use profanity."

"Only when necessary. Speaking of Towers, he wants me to set you up with a car phone."

"A what?"

"You heard me. He was trying to reach you yesterday before that remote from the Red Cross and almost went into coronary arrest when he couldn't get you."

"Terrific. I'll never be more than a quick seven digits away from the sweet sound of his voice."

Sympathy mixed with irony on Rosa's face. "Towers really is putting the pressure on you."

Jillian stashed her equipment. "The pressure's always on in this business." She turned toward the door. "Besides, it's a given. Radio men are a royal pain." *All radio men.*

"Say, don't run off. I thought maybe we could have lunch."

Jillian was tempted. When was the last time she'd shared a meal with one person instead of a crowd? "Can't. Sorry."

Rosa shrugged. "Say, what does J.T. stand for, anyway?"

"Why do you ask?"

"Let's just say I like having inside information. Tell me and I'll let you use my boat for a getaway weekend of depravity and debauchery."

Jillian grasped the doorknob and grinned. "Sorry, Rosa. Trade secret."

"Anybody ever told you you're very good at being evasive?"

"Almost every day," she said, surprised to realize just how much truth there was in her statement.

Jillian made up her mind, on the drive home, to stay away from the pool. She stripped off her knit dress and tossed it into the corner with the one from the day before, kicked her shoes into the back of the closet and peeled off her false eyelashes on the way to the shower.

But before she could turn on the water, the doorbell rang.

She froze. What stared back at her in the mirror was half Jillian, half J.T. She wrapped a towel around her flamboyant hair and studied the effect. Better. But still not completely safe.

The bell had rung twice more by the time she'd pulled on the worn terry-cloth robe hanging from a hook in the bathroom and made her way to the front door. The

pumping of her heart accelerated dangerously when Russ
Flynn greeted her in a white shirt and trim white tennis
shorts that showed off his dark tan and his solid muscles.

For one crazy, irrational moment, she thought he must
have come to tell her that her voice had given her away.

"Tennis, anyone?"

Apprehension constricted her throat. "No, thanks."

"That's just as well. I'm a lousy tennis player and I'd
hate to look bad before you even realize I'm your Prince
Charming."

"I think you have me confused with someone else. I'm
not looking for a Prince Charming."

"Sure, you are. You just don't know it yet." He peered
over her shoulder. "Mind if I come in?"

Then he walked past her without waiting for an answer, taking her so much by surprise that she didn't even
move to stop him. Panicked, she looked around to see
what might give her away. She had to get him out of here.

"Do you mind, Russ? I'm about to take a shower
and—"

"No, thanks, I've already had mine." He was walking
around the living room, taking in the cluttered book-
shelves and the stacks of newspapers littering the oversize coffee table. "But I'm a good back scrubber."

She edged behind the couch. "That wasn't an invitation. It was an explanation."

"Of why you're probably wearing nothing under-
neath that robe?"

She choked back a gasp. Russ grinned as he fingered
the spines of her books. Would he notice how many of
them were about entertainment?

"An explanation of why you have to leave."

"Oh." He turned away from the books and walked around the couch to stand beside her. "Then how about dinner tonight?"

"No. No, I can't." She huddled more tightly into her robe, succeeding only in allowing it to droop off her shoulder on one side. "I . . . I . . . I just can't." She looked away from the blue eyes that stared at her so patiently. "Really. I can't."

He reached out to rest his hand on her bared shoulder. His fingers felt alive against her skin, infusing it with a spark that flowed right from the tips of his fingers into the flesh of her shoulder. Her nipples hardened. She tensed against his touch and folded her arms tightly across her breasts.

"Why not?" he prodded. "Mama won't let you single-date yet? We could find another couple. Make it a nice, safe, double date."

He allowed one finger to trail lightly along the ridge of her shoulder, from the edge of her robe to the base of her neck, where she felt her pulse race. Warm. His fingers were warm on her ice-cold skin. He fingered a curl that straggled from beneath the towel covering her hair. What if the towel came loose? What color was the curl today? She struggled for breath.

"Don't be cute, Russ."

"Don't ask the impossible, Jill. I was born that way."

He was toying with her. That must be it. He had figured out who she was and this was all a ruse to pay her back. "I just . . . Can't we just be friends?"

Now, why in the world had she said that?

She couldn't meet his stare. His eyes told her he wanted more than just friendship; and she was certain, if she tried to stare him down, that her eyes would betray her guilt—just as her body had betrayed her desire at his touch.

"Can't friends have dinner together?"

"Sometime. But not now. I can't. That's all."

She turned away from him and headed for the door, but he caught her arm. His grip burned through her robe. She felt herself go moist. Hot and moist. He pulled her back toward him. The shock of their bodies pressed chest to chest weakened her. She melted into him even while she tried to remember why he mustn't see her reaction to him.

But it was too late for that, she knew, as her eyes drifted shut and she let herself lean into his hard, tempting body.

"What are you hiding from, Jill?"

His lips were close, his breath sweet and warm and urgent. She felt him stir against her. To hide the sound of the moan rising in her throat, she jerked away from his touch.

"What are you afraid of? Men in general? Or me in particular?"

"I think you'd better leave." She made her voice cold, in hopes it would compensate for how obviously she had been affected by his nearness. What would she do if he didn't leave? If, instead, he peeled back the edges of her robe? Lowered his head and . . .

"Yourself?" he persisted.

Damn him all to hell and back. She marched to the door and held it open. "Goodbye, Russ."

He left, grinning confidently, taking a moment to pull the collar of her robe securely around her throat before he made his way out the door—so in control. She hated him.

When he was safely locked on the other side of her condo door, she sagged against it, her heart thudding painfully. Every part of her pulsated with a desire to undo the last few moments, to act out a new ending to the encounter.

When she'd finally calmed down, she peered between the curtains to discover Russ standing where she'd left him, staring at her door. She felt, as she let the curtain drop into place, as if she were going back into hiding.

Her whisper rang with bitterness. "Well, aren't you?"

AT FIRST, HAVING HIS very own, honest-to-goodness mystery woman had seemed like fun to Russ. But the fun of playing cat and mouse with Jillian Joyner was wearing thin.

The problem was, he couldn't get her out of his mind. Just the way it had been with Lonnie, he reminded himself brutally as he swapped street clothes for gym shorts and a T-shirt in the locker room of the Youth Center.

He cursed himself. He'd been trying like the devil not to compare Jillian and Lonnie. But it was impossible not to draw parallels. He'd made a fool of himself over Lonnie for the same reasons he was going to make a fool of himself over Jillian.

He'd been attracted to the FSU assistant professor for the same reasons he was now attracted to Jillian. They were both smart, both educated, classy—all the things that Russ knew deep in his soul he was not.

Even as he went through the motions of starting up a game of basketball with the kids in the gym, Russ couldn't stop berating himself. No, Russ might be intrigued by Jillian's brains and class, but he was still a farm boy who'd hardly been able to muster the smarts to finish high school. He belonged with the flighty little airheads who pursued him, not with women like Jillian. The six months he and Lonnie had been engaged had proven that. Faculty mixers and sedate little cocktail parties with her psych-department colleagues had been Russ's downfall. Every time he'd opened his mouth in Lonnie's circle of friends, his nervousness had taken the form of one inane comment after another. He had embarrassed Lonnie once too often—until the night she'd said, "Why don't you learn to keep your mouth shut? College faculty aren't interested in playing straight man in one of your routines, Russ."

And here he was, pulling the same thing with Jillian, when he should have learned his lesson. But he couldn't seem to help himself. He wanted her. And he'd forgotten the frustration of one-sided crushes. Worse, his self-confidence was taking one whale of a beating. His easy grin and even easier wisecracks served as his cover, as his measure of self-confidence with women who were no intellectual challenge—the kind of women he'd limited himself to since Lonnie.

And now, with Jillian—with another woman who really was classy and smart and something more he hadn't quite pinned down—the usual tricks weren't working.

With a frustrated grunt, Russ heaved the basketball toward the hoop and wasn't surprised when it met with a disappointed groan from his kids.

"Good job, Flynn." Ron Costner, a WKIX sportscaster who had teamed up with the other half of the youths at the center this afternoon, ragged him. "You've got a great air ball."

"Come on, dude," Howie said, slapping Russ on the back. "Get in the game. We're not gonna let these punks whip us."

The punks whipped them.

But André's chipped front tooth was revealed in a big smile anyway as he shoved the basketball at Russ's midsection. "Man, we're not gonna pick up your option if you don't get on the ball."

You and everyone else, Russ thought.

"Give him a break," Howie protested, rubbing a towel over his soft brown curls. He grinned shyly. "Whaddaya expect? He's so old."

Russ groaned in response to Howie's ribbing and headed to the sideline, taking care not to look down at the gleaming white sweat socks rising up out of his two young friends' ragged athletic shoes.

Next, new shoes, he vowed to himself. He really got satisfaction from being a part of the lives of the boys at the center. More satisfaction, really, than he'd ever felt in fifteen years of radio work. Maybe if he stuck with these kids, he could make sure a few of them grew up minus the insecurities that kept him so tied up in knots. That would mean a heck of a lot more than another six years of winning the ratings war.

"Hope you're not planning on turning pro anytime soon," Ron said, following Russ to the sideline and slipping off his damp T-shirt.

"Hey, I look a lot better when you aren't out there." Russ dropped onto the bench and mopped his face with a towel. His lanky co-worker had been a local high-school star a decade earlier and had seemed destined for a pro career until he injured a knee while playing basketball for Duke University.

"I just like to show you up."

Before Russ could reply, Howie walked over to join them. Russ could see the hero worship in Howie's sharp black eyes as he peered up at Ron. "Mr. Costner? I wondered if I could have your autograph?"

Howie's shy request was the icebreaker. After Ron had signed Howie's T-shirt, most of the others in the gym came over for similar attention.

Pleased, Russ remembered how important it had been to him, the first time an announcer from the tiny local station in Santiago had paid attention to him. And he'd had a lot more going for himself than these kids did. He'd never had the advantages money could buy, but he'd had a stable family. Most of these kids would swap every new pair of Air Jordan sneakers in town for the kind of family Russ had taken for granted.

Yeah, it should come as no shock that the few hours a week he spent here felt so much better than all the glory he got for being on the air.

Studying his now treasured T-shirt, Howie dropped onto the bench beside Russ. "Hey, Russ?" Howie spoke softly and looked up to reassure himself that no one in the group was paying attention. "Just thought you'd want to know. My mom's home."

Russ wasn't certain the relief he felt was justified. Howie's mother had left home one morning two weeks ago and failed to come home for dinner. Nothing new, Russ was sad to have learned. But, terrified of being torn away from his family or getting his mother in trouble, Howie had pleaded with Russ not to notify the authorities. Smoothing over the rough spots was the role Howie had accepted as his in life.

As Howie had shuffled between the homes of an aunt and his aging great-grandmother, Russ worried if he'd made the right decision. At times, he'd been tempted to snatch the teen—who already felt torn between his Cuban and black heritage—from his unstable environment and take him home with him.

The strength of that protective urge had astonished Russ. "Are you glad she's back?"

Howie twisted the crystal stud earring glittering in his right ear. "Sure. She said she just had to get away for a while. That's all. I can dig that."

Despite the bravado of his words, Russ saw the hurt confusion in Howie's eyes. He sometimes felt like the lives of the boys at the center were time bombs, and that the job of defusing them one by one was overwhelming. Still, he was glad the station had taken on the project, and even more gratified that he was a part of it.

"Did you tell her how you felt when she went away?" Russ already knew the answer to that. Howie was always careful to say and do the right thing. Never Rock The Boat—that was Howie's motto.

Howie shrugged off the suggestion. "It's okay, Russ. I understand how it is."

Russ wanted to tell Howie he didn't have to be perfect, didn't have to carry the world's problems on his shoulders. He wanted to tell him he could be more like André if he wanted—angry sometimes, and demanding that the world give him a fair shake. But the compulsion to be perfect, so the world would accept him, was Howie's burden. Russ understood that. And he understood he couldn't push too hard for him to change.

"So, how's the algebra coming along? Need another session with the books?"

"Aw, man, do we have to?"

"How are you going to be a lawyer if you don't get to college? And how are you going to get to college if you pull a flag in algebra?"

The way Howie looked down at his shoes, Russ knew he was embarrassed that he'd ever revealed his secret dream. "You really think I can go to law school?"

"If you want it bad enough to work for it."

While the others finished getting autographs from the sportscaster, Russ cajoled Howie into setting up another tutoring session. And when the last of the admiring boys wandered off, Ron grinned. "Sorry about that."

"That's the price of running with a sports hero."

"Yeah, that's me." Ron dropped onto the bench beside Russ. "Listen, I'm not sure your heart was in this today. What's up, pal? You've seemed a little deflated lately."

Russ shoved his towel into his gym bag, emblazoned with the WKIX logo. "Really?"

Ron snorted and punched Russ on the shoulder. "Don't try to con me, pal. You've been one gloomy puppy for the past few days. So, give. What's up?"

Shrugging, Russ, zipped his bag. He wasn't ready to admit, even to himself, that he'd been moody because of a woman who wouldn't give him the time of day. He'd written Jillian off—but only because she'd written him off. At least, that's what she seemed to want him to think—for some unfathomable reason. Yet, he'd seen the desire in her face, felt it tremble through her body.

Hadn't he?

Perhaps he'd been right from the beginning: this woman was too complicated.

A glance up at Ron's inquisitive face told him it was time for diversionary tactics.

"You heard the new morning jock on WFLA?"

"The Tallahassee Lassie?" Ron let out a low whistle. "Who hasn't? Is that what's bugging you?"

Russ brought his feet up onto the bench and stretched, allowing his silence to stand as a response to Ron's conclusion. After all, it really wasn't a lie. Especially since that phone hookup. Something about Jammin' J.T. had drawn him to her. Something about her voice intrigued him.

"Don't sweat it, Flynn," Ron said, reassuringly. "She'll be hot for about twenty minutes, then fizzle out."

"Don't bet on it," Russ warned. "I've taped a couple of her shows. She's good. She's..." He paused, stumped.

"She's what, man?"

How could he explain that something about the woman excited him? That kind of confession would put him in the same category as all the groupies who trailed after radio people. "I don't know. She's just special."

"Guess it's tough, having serious competition for the first time in six years."

What made it really tough, Russ had to admit, was his preoccupation with his mystery woman. Jammin' J.T., he could handle. But thanks to Jillian Joyner, he could barely concentrate on putting together material for his show every morning.

And that was even scarier than the thought of a ratings battle with the sharp-witted Tallahassee Lassie.

RUSS HAD STAYED AWAY from Jillian for what seemed like weeks now. He stopped to count. Well, days, anyway. Ever since she'd turned down his dinner invitation with no explanation. That had really steamed him.

Forget it, he told himself, wandering aimlessly through his condo in search of some distraction. He thumbed through the TV schedule, then tuned in to a documentary on public television. But he couldn't sit still long enough to watch.

Then he stretched out in the recliner to read the day's newspapers. But his brain was too wired to take in what he was reading.

Maybe a swim would help. At this hour of night, no doubt his mystery lady was locked in her tower and he'd have the pool to himself. The exercise would wear him out, he hoped.

But ten minutes later, when he reached the gate to the pool area, he saw Jillian sitting on the side, her worn jeans rolled up to her knees, her feet dangling in the water. Her hair was loose, falling in waves to her waist. He was almost upon her before she was aware of his presence.

"So, you do get your feet wet."

Her head jerked around at his voice and he was treated to a fleeting hint of pleased surprise before she managed to assume her usual cool mask. But he knew what he'd seen—no matter how fleeting. He wasn't so inexperienced with women, that he would misread such an obvious signal.

But why was she trying so hard to scramble the transmission?

"Hello, Russ."

He dropped the towel on the end of a lounge chair and remained standing over her. "And you do come out at night. I thought maybe you weren't allowed out after dark. Maybe—"

She jumped to her feet, grabbing her sandals from the tile as she turned to face him. "Stop it, Russ. I can't handle your needling tonight."

As she brushed past him, he reached out and took hold of her wrist. She turned back in astonishment, her hair swinging softly. And now that he had her, he wasn't sure what he intended.

"Don't go, Jill. I've missed you."

Her face filled with confusion and she looked down. Her breasts, not as tightly bound as they'd been by her maillot, rose and fell heavily under the flowing print blouse that topped her jeans. A spasm of desire gripped Russ. He made an effort not to notice their ripe fullness.

"I ... I missed you, too, Russ. But ..." She tugged her hand away. Instead of loosening his grip, he tightened it.

"Then stay."

"N-no. It's late. I ..."

He took a step closer and found her other wrist with his other hand. Her wrists were tiny, the bones fragile. He felt the pulse there, like the frantic flutter of a bird's wings—a captive bird. The tip of her tongue flickered out to moisten her lips. Her gaze rose to his in silent supplication.

"I've always wanted to kiss a stranger," he said softly, pulling her body into his. She was soft and round against him and, instead of tensing as he had feared she would, she seemed to melt into him. "Someone I didn't know. A total stranger."

As she looked into his eyes, her coolness was now completely gone. "I'm not a stranger. You're in the wrong fantasy," she whispered.

"Oh, no, I'm not."

He lowered his lips toward hers and waited, but she made no move to resist. His mouth brushed hers tentatively at first, waiting for her response, struggling to keep his own in check. When she didn't pull away, he released one wrist at a time, and slipped his hands around her waist. He felt her fingers tremble as they slid slowly up his chest. His tongue flicked out to taste the corners of her mouth. When he heard her breath catch, he tightened his hold on her and crushed her breasts against him. His mouth covered hers, hungrily, and she met his tongue with her own.

He growled as her fingers grazed his nipples. Her thighs, as full as her breasts, leaned into his, and the softness of her belly ground into him, seeking and finding his hardness. He filled his hands with her buttocks and pulled her more tightly against his erection.

Like a drowning man, he pulled his lips from hers, taking in gulps of air as he buried his face in her hair, against her neck, against her cheek. Soft moans escaped her lips as she cradled his head in her hands and held him close.

"Come in the water with me," he whispered, pulling away long enough to look into her dazed eyes. She nodded. They loosened their tight embrace long enough to move toward the pool.

"What are we doing?" she murmured, her voice fuzzy with desire.

"Fantasizing." Yet, when he felt her hand tense in his, he released her.

"No. I— This is a mistake. This won't work, Russ. It just won't work."

"It's a fantasy, Jillian. That's all. It doesn't have to be anything more. I won't ask anything more." His heart began to thud frantically, more in desperation than desire.

She backed off, her eyes so wide with fear that it tore at his gut. He wanted to reassure her, but realized he didn't have the foggiest notion what to say that wouldn't scare her away.

It was too late, anyway. She turned suddenly and ran. Clenching his fists, Russ stared at the pool. No simple swim would give him rest tonight. He swore angrily and dove in.

4

JILLIAN PULLED OUT into traffic and barely noticed the approaching car swerve to miss her.

Like the traffic zipping by on Tennessee Street, virtually everything had zipped by unnoticed for days. Instead, she obsessively replayed Russ's kiss—remembering the feel of his lips on hers, and the devastating effect of his kiss.

The ringing of the car phone jolted her back to reality.

As she picked up the contraption Towers had installed to aggravate her, she slammed on her brakes to avoid running the red light she'd been too preoccupied to heed.

"What now?" she barked into the receiver, expecting another ten-minute barrage of ideas for creating Jammin' J.T., Superstar.

"Growing sweeter every day, I see."

"Mother." She groaned softly.

"The welcome in your voice is a blessing to me in my old age, darling."

Jillian grunted to keep from laughing. Old age was still years away from catching up with Audrey Tate. Her five decades had been kind to the comic actress. Her plastic surgeon had been even kinder. Jillian smiled in spite of herself. In another ten years, her flighty mother would no doubt look younger than her daughter. "Doddering again, are you?"

"Wouldn't dream of it. You know your father hates it when I dodder."

Jillian bit back a caustic retort. After parading four stepfathers through her daughter's life, Audrey still couldn't remember that Jillian didn't call them Father— *wouldn't* call them Father. Not since that first time when Audrey had made Jillian hug her new husband and call him Daddy for the benefit of the news reporters hovering around the courthouse.

So convenient, Audrey had pointed out, getting married at the same courthouse where her first divorce had just been finalized.

"What is it, Mother?"

Forcing herself to pay attention to the still-unfamiliar Tallahassee streets as she drove toward home, Jillian tried to squelch her uneasiness. Audrey never called simply to chat.

"Is Tallahassee nice, darling?"

"Lovely. What is it, Mother?"

The pause to build dramatic tension was effective. Audrey's timing was always perfect. "It's your father."

"You mean Henry." Henry was husband number five. Jillian's real father had faded into obscurity years ago. Or had been hounded into it. The media hadn't wanted to let go of the quiet financial analyst who had lived a few years in the eye of Hurricane Audrey. Jillian hadn't heard from him in almost two decades, since he'd finally shaken off the publicity and made a quiet life for himself.

"Yes. Henry. He's trying to ruin my career."

"I see."

All of Audrey's husbands had tried to "ruin her career" at one time or another. Jillian had often speculated how different her life might have been if one of them had succeeded. But Audrey's star had shone brightly for decades, ever since she'd first costarred on her vaude-ville father's radio show as a child during World War II. Her squeaky little voice had won the hearts of America. And later, Technicolor and Panavision had made it possible for her bright red hair and luminous green eyes to capture America all over again as an adult. A klutzy, endearing screwball, Audrey Tate had starred opposite one Hollywood leading man after another during a thirty-year period starting in the late fifties. Only during the last couple of years had Audrey's age caught up with her, making good roles tough to come by.

Audrey's career had taken a back seat to nothing—goodness knows, her husbands had tried. They'd wanted extended honeymoons, when she belonged to them and not the press. They'd wanted a few weeks a year when she wasn't working on location. They'd wanted to go to Hollywood parties without hearing another rumor that Audrey had grown *so very close* to you-know-who while she was filming in North Carolina.

Jillian could have told them it was futile to expect Audrey to care about anything or anyone more than her career. It wasn't that she was heartless or cold; she was simply self-centered, with the naive self-absorption of one who had been in the spotlight since infancy.

Jillian sighed. "What's Henry doing to ruin your career, Mother?"

"I've had the most wonderful movie offer—and you know how long it's been since I've had a movie offer. Do you know how hard it is for a woman my age to get a good movie role?"

Jillian sighed, cursing the bad luck that had made her an only child. Audrey's trials and tribulations would be so much easier to swallow if they could be spread around.

"So I'm wondering if it wouldn't be better to separate. Just for a while. To see if—"

"Mother. Not again."

"Now, Jillie, I'm not talking about divorce. Just some time apart. To let things cool off."

"Why don't you try to work this out with Henry, Mother?"

"How *is* Tallahassee this time of year? Is it dreadfully humid?"

"Dreadfully. Unbearably. Eye makeup melts right off your face." Audrey, here? No. It couldn't happen. The old familiar feeling of doom descended on Jillian. "Mother, Henry is a wonderful man. An understanding man. Talk to him. You can work this out. I know you can."

"Do you really think so?"

"Of course, I do."

Although Audrey promised to try, Jillian had little faith in her mother's vows. Vows were not something Audrey took very seriously. Audrey took punch lines seriously. And crow's feet. Not vows.

Jillian turned her car between the palm trees at the entrance to the Wendover Court parking lot. Just how had her father managed to disappear so completely? Why couldn't she manage to do likewise? If he had turned his back on Audrey, why couldn't she?

"Because everybody loves Audrey," she muttered to herself. "Crazy, funny Audrey."

And it was true. In spite of everything, she loved her mother dearly. But that didn't keep her from being rattled by Audrey's call as she prepared to turn into her parking space. Then she noticed someone getting off a motorcycle a few spaces down. Always worried about being spotted on her home turf in her Jammin' J.T. garb, she slowed down.

It was Russ. He was looking in her direction, pausing to remove his helmet. She knew he couldn't see her in the darkness. But if he came toward her as she pulled in, it would be all over. By now, even Russ Flynn must know what his competition looked like. And if he discovered that Jammin' J.T. and his mousy-looking neighbor were one and the same, the masquerade would be finished.

Then, even Rosa might have trouble keeping the local news media from hounding her to death. Her secret would be out. Even if Audrey kept her precious turned-up nose out of Tallahassee, Jillian's quiet life would be at an end.

And if Audrey showed up, too . . . She couldn't even bear to think about that.

Without hesitating, Jillian pressed the gas pedal and zoomed out of the lot. She circled the block six times before she crept cautiously back into the deserted parking area.

RUSS ROLLED HIS SLEEVES down and buttoned the cuffs as he headed down the hall, satisfied that another morning show had gone well.

"Good show, pal." Ron's voice from the newsroom halted Russ. "I liked the baseball bit."

"Thanks." He stepped into the sound studio and dropped into a chair. Draping his headset around his neck, he wished he'd enjoyed the show more himself. "Thought you'd like that one. How about shooting some hoops over at the center this afternoon? I've got to run by the community college around lunchtime—we've got a meeting about the broadcast curriculum they're developing. After that, I figure I'll need something physical to work out the aggravation. How about it?"

"Only if you're with it today. I don't like wasting my time on stiffs who can't hit the side of a barn. You're not still worried about 'FLA, are you?"

"Naw. The way I figure it—"

The studio door creaked as it opened. Russ looked around to see Tony Covington standing over them, wearing his best station manager's glare. "Flynn. How about taking a few minutes from this little *tête-à-tête* to step into my office?"

Without waiting for an answer, Tony turned and stalked away. Mockingly, Ron held his quivering hands up in front of him. "On second thought, pal, maybe you'd better start brushing up your résumé. Boss man looked steamed about something."

"Guess I'd better snap to."

More annoyed than worried about whatever had Tony in a lather, Russ arranged to meet Ron at the center after lunch, then headed for Tony's office.

Tony scowled as Russ entered. Russ resigned himself to yet another of those tense sessions that were inevitable in the pressure-cooker world of radio.

Tony didn't speak for several seconds. When he did, his tone was ominous. "I'm not happy, Flynn."

Trying to estimate how long it would take for the station manager to vent whatever was sticking in his craw, Russ willed himself to remain calm.

"I'm not happy about WFLA, Flynn." Tony paused and was disappointed—Russ could tell—that the disc jockey hadn't jumped in to apologize or make excuses. "Everywhere I turn, I'm hit between the eyes by their new morning personality. Everywhere you find a crowd of people these days, Jammin' J.T. is right smack in the middle of the mob. Every time I open the newspaper, I see another picture of that damn woman."

Tony frowned, then continued. "I know you've topped the ratings for a long time. And we want to keep it that way." He leaned forward. "You know, I was at a breakfast meeting at the club yesterday and the people at the next table were talking about her. Spoiled my grits and ham, I can tell you that. But that's not the worst of it."

Russ waited to hear the worst of it.

"My wife—my *wife,* mind you—listens to her. Caught her at it this morning. I forgot my briefcase and had to go back after it and caught her—she'd already switched stations. Said she did it every day. Can you believe it? My own wife!"

"That's a low blow, Tony." Russ found it next to impossible to keep his voice serious. "Grounds for divorce, I'd say. Or maybe justifiable homicide."

"I'll give you justifiable homicide, Flynn, if you play wise guy with me this morning." Tony's jaw jutted belligerently. "I'm dead serious. We're not going to take this lying down."

"We're not?"

"We certainly are not." Tony slammed a fist down on the pile of papers that cluttered his desk. "We're going to fight back. Starting tonight."

"Tonight?"

"With the Junior League gala. I want you there." He tossed a folder across the desk at Russ. "There's a schedule. I want you all over this town in the next few months."

Staring at the folder, Russ sat up straighter. "The Junior League gala? Personal appearances? Tony, you know I've got more on my plate than I can handle already. With the Youth Center and the college committee and that theater group you wanted me to direct. We agreed more than a year ago that I should limit that kind of purely promotional appearance—save them for community events that had the most emotional appeal, so that—"

"That was last year, Flynn. That was before the Tallahassee Lassie hit town." Tony gave his tie a frustrated jerk. "I'm not having some flighty dame breeze into town and snatch our listeners right out from under us. Wherever Jammin' J.T. is, I want you there. With bells on."

AFTER FIDGETING THROUGH the college-curriculum meeting Russ decided to forgo the Youth Center that afternoon. He wouldn't be there in spirit. Besides, the kids were way too sharp to be fooled. So he made excuses to Ron and headed home.

As well, he felt a little guilty admitting to himself that the main reason he'd spent so much time there in recent days was to keep his mind off his unfriendly new neighbor.

That kiss you stole wasn't a bit unfriendly, pal, he told himself as his bike roared into his parking space in front of the salmon-colored stucco condominium complex.

As always when he recalled their go-for-broke kiss, Russ got stirred up. Furious at himself for his lack of control, he yanked his helmet off. The air was heavy with humidity and smelled of rainfall. Tallahassee's famous afternoon monsoon season must be arriving early this year.

He'd only gone two steps toward his building when he saw her. She was opening the trunk of her car, one of those sporty jobs with lots of chrome and fast lines—another clue to the mystery lady, a clue that didn't fit with the rest of the puzzle at all. It was red and it was a ragtop and it looked like anyone but shy and retiring little Jillian Joyner.

It occurred to him, as he watched her heft a bag of groceries onto one hip, that it looked a lot like the woman he'd kissed: a woman with fire.

He'd felt the fire. He didn't doubt its existence for a moment. She had been as ready as he'd been to lose herself in the heat that had engulfed them.

But something else had been stronger.

Before he realized it, his feet were taking him toward her. *It's time for action. After all, she can't turn me down forever. Can she?*

As Russ stepped up to her car, Jillian froze, her hand on the trunk. The look that flashed over her face told him he was right. She couldn't reject him forever. But that fleeting openness was quickly replaced by her familiar guardedness.

"I know what you're thinking," he said, forcing a breezy grin as he retrieved two of the bags she'd set down on the pavement. "How fortuitous! What timing! How like fate to throw us together like this, just when you were wondering if you would ever see me again."

She glared at him. She pushed her straw hat back on her head and gave him a hostile look. He kept grinning.

"Russ, don't start up with me."

"Okay, how about this? Just when you were speculating how you were going to get four bags of groceries upstairs with only two arms. You must have the winning lottery ticket, ma'am. I just happen to have two extra arms."

"Russ, I'm not in the—"

He snapped his fingers. "I knew it. You're not in the mood. I've got just the thing. For your mood. A cure-all for the cranky. Medication for the moody. A party."

"Cranky? I am not— What did you say? A party?" Her irritation was replaced by incredulity.

Russ had to sympathize with her. He was a bit incredulous himself that he had the nerve to act so cocky when she kept cutting him dead—no matter how unconvincing she'd been. But it was the only way he had the nerve to approach her. That way, it might not hurt so much when she made another hasty escape.

But he was too obsessed not to go after her.

"A party." He was obsessed with the quick wit he'd noticed right away. Obsessed with the shyness he'd picked up the second time they met. And definitely obsessed with the hint of something more, something hidden, something she guarded jealously. Something that had burst to the surface when she'd bought this snazzy little ragtop. Now he recognized another layer of her personality—a will so strong she could even fight the undeniable attraction between them. That strength appealed to him as much as everything else he'd slowly pieced together about this mysteriously evasive woman. Yes, he was obsessed, pure and simple. He cleared his throat and tried to remember what he'd been saying. "Right. A party. You know. Music. Food. Spirits. Debauchery."

He paused for a moment, thinking about past Junior League galas. "Well, maybe not debauchery. But all the other stuff."

Her gaze lingered on his face, studying his eyes. When she bit down on her full upper lip, he reached out to touch her. Was her skin as smooth, as warm as he remembered?

Before his hand could connect with her arm, she moved. With clipped, jerky movements, she gathered up two bags. He grabbed the other two.

"You'll like these people." He followed her down the sidewalk and up the stairs to her condo, trying to hold on to his cavalier tone. But he knew it was too late. Again. She was walking away from him. Again.

"I won't like 'these people.'" She unlocked her front door and stopped inside to set her bags on the floor in the foyer. Then blocked the doorway.

"Sure, you will. We're talking major-league phonies. It's your big chance to—"

"Russ." The word was authoritarian. When he met her gaze, he realized she was staring over his shoulder. "I am *not* going out with you. Not tonight. Not tomorrow night. Not ever. You've clever. You're charming. You're hard to resist, but . . ."

He took advantage of her moment's hesitation to move in closer. They were toe-to-toe. She had to look up or direct her conversation into his chest.

"I'm a swell guy, but you have to do your hair," he snapped, only acknowledging as the words spilled out that he couldn't keep up the funny-guy routine any longer. "I'm a real sweetheart, but your parakeet is expecting you home early tonight. I'm every woman's dream, but you'd rather make love to your pillow. Is that it, Jillian?"

Her face was flushed with emotion. With anger to match his own. "That's right."

Frustration fueled his anger. He shoved the grocery bags into her arms. How could he hope to reach someone who was so walled in? He wheeled around and started for the stairs. Halfway down, he called out to her.

"Someday, nobody's going to bother anymore. Then what?"

He drew meager satisfaction from the fact that her shoulders sagged as she closed her front door.

THE MUSIC WAS A LIFELESS imitation of a swing band. The hors d'oeuvres were elegant and rich—oysters Rockefeller, pâté de foie gras, caviar.

Russ tasted the caviar and grimaced. Yep. He still hated it. He had hated it the first time he ate it, in his one-and-only college world-lit class right after the midterm exam on Dostoyevsky and Tolstoy, the one and only quarter he'd attended Florida State. In deference to those who kept insisting caviar was an acquired taste, he kept tasting it. It had worked with olives and avocado. But not caviar.

The caviar wasn't the only thing leaving a bitter taste in his mouth. Russ still hated the plastic smiles, the gushing greetings, and the ostentatious ambience of charity fund-raisers. Why didn't they donate the money they wasted on their gowns to whatever charity they were ostensibly raising money for?

You're just in a rotten mood! And it has nothing to do with your noble motives when it comes to charity.

He looked around, curious if there were any likely candidates in the crowd to take his mind off Jillian. Consolation. That's what he needed. A smooth white shoulder to cry on.

"Russ!"

With a press of her fragrant cheek against his, one of the glittering Junior Leaguers appropriated her celebrity guest and proceeded to press him into duty. For the next half hour, Russ smiled, Russ pumped flesh, Russ displayed his wit and his charm and his boyish smile.

He also kept his eye out for a woman who could help him forget how rotten Jillian had made him feel this afternoon. But they were all too tall. Too svelte. Too lacquered and painted and spangled. Just like all the women he'd been so careful to cultivate in recent years. Women who were too plastic to elicit much emotion.

Russ sighed and endured another five minutes with a real-estate agent who was entertaining the idea of running for county office. What, he wanted to know, did Russ see as the pressing issues that would move the voters at election time?

Just as the would-be politician was driving home his point about zoning regulations, a ripple of laughter near the champagne fountain distracted Russ. Casually, so his companion wouldn't guess that it took more than zoning regulations to get him cranked up, Russ glanced over in the direction of the rumble.

There she was. His competition. Jammin' J.T. The flaming red curls, in an unruly pile atop her head, the silver lamé halter that left her smooth, milky back bare to the waist, the skintight, lace-trimmed leggings, the makeup that bordered on the bizarre. It was her in the flesh—Jammin' J.T.

Russ looked away. But as he listened to the real-estate agent, he found himself compelled to take just another peek.

Yes, she really was as outrageous as she looked in photographs. Although, up close, she radiated a certain vulnerability and an undeniable sensuality. Something in the eyes, and that soft pout of a mouth.

He looked away again. But as Russ opened his mouth to form some encouraging comment to his companion, something about the Tallahassee Lassie tugged at him. Against his better judgment, he looked a third time.

At that moment, she turned in his direction, smiling mischievously. Her smile froze in stunned horror at the same moment his did.

Russ finally realized why his elusive neighbor had been so elusive.

5

NOW JILLIAN KNEW exactly how it would feel to find herself naked, with every microphone and TV camera in the world pointed in her direction.

She wished she could vanish, disappear. Her gaze skittered around the room, looking for an escape route. But the ballroom was so crowded that reaching a door—quickly and invisibly—seemed almost impossible. She was trapped. Completely and utterly trapped.

She glanced over at Russ, who looked just as nakedly vulnerable as she felt. His eyes darkened with a hurt she knew too well.

Her guilt was so overwhelming that it overrode her compulsion to flee, to seek cover. She had done this to herself, yes. And she'd done it to Russ, too.

She ached with the need to rush over, put her hand on his arm, to explain.

"Why, J.T.," Rosa drawled in her ear, "I do believe you've caught the eye of your competition. And if I'm not mistaken, he looks . . . staggered."

Jillian leaned toward Rosa and hissed in her ear, "I'm leaving."

She started walking, without a backward glance at the startled socialites around her. Rosa caught up with her and tugged on her arm.

"We're in my car, remember? What are you talking about?"

"Leaving. Taking a hike. Blowing this joint." Jillian mustered a tough glare in response to Rosa's smug grin. "Going home. Got it?"

"Are you crazy?"

"Yes. Now, follow me, pal. There's a break in the teeming masses right there, and if we hurry..."

"I think I'm enjoying this. Jammin' J.T. in a tizzy. Ms. Control loses control. I'm glad I'm here to witness this for myself."

Rosa's satisfaction was justified. Jillian had shrugged off her friendship every time it was offered. Why shouldn't she be enjoying this little demonstration of just how uncool J.T. could be?

Desperate measures, that's what this calls for. "Come on. Now. If we leave now, I'll...I'll...tell you what J.T. stands for."

Rosa smiled serenely and shook her head. "No, I think this is worth a lot more than that. If you leave now, I'll have to explain it to Towers. For that much aggravation, I think—"

"To hell with Towers." She took Rosa by the arm and tried to wend her way through the throng. "I'm out of here."

Rosa rooted herself to the floor and crossed her arms across the crisp linen of her suit. "Not until you tell me why."

Jillian turned toward Rosa, groping for an explanation. Her explanation was purposefully making its way in their direction. Urgency rapidly escalated to panic.

"Because I turn into a pumpkin at nine o'clock, that's why. Now stop expecting me to be reasonable, and come on."

"If I let you fly out of here now, just when Russ Flynn shows up, Towers will wave his wand and turn us both into . . ."

Jillian glanced frantically over Rosa's shoulder. "I'm warning you, Rosa. In another thirty seconds, the ball gown disappears. Rags and cinders. That's all you'll have left."

"If you'll just tell me . . ."

Too late. The clock had just struck midnight.

"Well, well, well. If it isn't the Dynamic Duo from 'FLA.'" Russ's voice was like the icicles that had dripped from the upstairs eaves outside her bedroom window in Connecticut—sharp, hard and so icy cold they might never thaw.

"Long time no see, Flynn," Rosa said.

Jillian was only vaguely aware of the speculative look on Rosa's face as she surveyed the two disc jockeys. She was more aware of Russ's scrutiny. She was more aware that he now held the power to unmask her. She was more aware that the vulnerability she'd imagined in his face just moments before was gone.

"You two have never met, I take it?" Rosa's voice revealed that she suspected otherwise, but Jillian ignored her accusation.

"Not . . . officially." But without waiting for introductions, Russ reached out and captured Jillian's wrist in a move that was disconcertingly familiar. "You'll excuse us, won't you, Ms. Miguel? They're playing our song."

Jillian opened her mouth to protest, but Russ shook his head to quiet her. "Wouldn't you hate to cause a scene, right here in front of all these nice people?"

"You wouldn't dare." She spat out the words from between clenched teeth. Anger leavened her fear and the heat from the touch of his hand made it rise.

He smiled—and backed toward the dance floor. She followed. And Rosa's wry voice followed her through the crowd: "Don't trip over your glass slipper."

He pulled her close against him. His dinner jacket felt rough against her bare arms. She wanted to speak, but she could scarcely breathe, let alone form words. His body, swaying to the beat of the music, impelled her to move with him.

"Don't I know you from somewhere?" The innocuously banal pickup line was delivered without the slightest attempt to hide the sarcasm in his voice.

Jillian looked up into his eyes, then away, scorched by his anger—and something else. Something that frightened her more than the anger. "Russ, don't do this."

"Ah, you *do* know me. But I can't seem to place you. The face is familiar—but . . ." He paused as if to consider. "Was it Paris, the summer of '87?"

"I'm sorry." But the hastily snapped words, she knew, conveyed no remorse. She was sorry for that, too. "But surely you can understand."

His arm tightened against her back. When she looked up, his eyes had grown stormy with anger. "Understand? Understand what, Jillian? Or should I call you J.T.? What do all your *intimate* friends call you, Jillian?"

The sneering hostility in the final words cut her and she pulled away. "Leave me alone. Do you get it now, Russ? I just want you to leave me alone."

Before he could react, she wheeled around. Her spike heels made it hard, though, to stalk off. And they didn't even give her enough height to easily scan the crush of people for Rosa.

Dazed by a swirl of conflicting emotions, Jillian tried to push through the crowd. She squeezed between high, black-coated backs, frustrated that she couldn't see the door, couldn't see the windows. All she could see was people, so she didn't even know whether she was moving in the right direction or merely getting caught in the crush.

Dodging elbows, she brushed past trays of drinks balanced on the hands of white-coated servers. Sequins and black ties seemed to block her path at every turn. Every space that opened before her seemed to close up as soon as she took two steps toward it.

"What luck! J.T., I've been hoping all night to get a chance..."

She looked up into the bespectacled eyes of the local reporter who'd been hounding Rosa to set up an interview. Without acknowledging the reporter, Jillian rapidly backed away, in the process bumping into a couple standing behind her.

"Excuse me." She smiled apologetically, then she continued to maneuver through the hordes of partyers. Desperate to find Rosa, she stood on the tips of her toes to scan the crowd. Where was Rosa? And where was the damn exit?

She turned, and came up against Russ's crisp white shirt. He smiled. She felt raw panic.

"I think you're avoiding me tonight, sweetness," he whispered, draping an arm around her shoulders.

She held her breath, ducked away and turned in the other direction. Then, before she could get her bearings, there he was at her side once again, whispering in her ear.

"Maybe you've got the right idea. Let's get out of this mob. Go back to my place. I have a chilled bottle of . . ."

Jillian darted away again, leaving him grinning that unpleasant grin that clearly indicated seduction was actually the *last* thing on his mind. How long, she wondered, would it take to get a cab? She put as much distance as possible between them, cursing her decision to ride with Rosa.

She cursed her decision to come at all. Cursed a lifetime of decisions that had brought her nothing but anxiety and regret.

Only this time, the regret was triggered by more than just anxiety. This time, she felt as if something had shattered, something that would never be the same again. If she hadn't come to this party, the different parts of her life would still be safely tucked away in their own little compartments. But this time, there was Russ. And Russ seemed to have changed everything. As if . . .

She was too confused to think coherently. To get her bearings, she paused at the hors d'oeuvres table, smack in the middle of the room. All she knew was that right now the remorse she felt over betraying Russ the way she had was more powerful than her dread of public scrutiny. If she could make Russ understand, then maybe—

"You mean you can eat in that outfit?"

Russ's voice was close to her ear, teasing and tempting. She turned to face him, automatically taking a step backward. He was too near—far too near, she thought, as she observed the self-confidence shining in his eyes.

Had it been only her imagination—that vulnerable look in his eyes? Only wishful thinking?

"I would have thought that one more bite of food and you'd—" his gaze lowered to the cleavage visible above the low neckline of her clinging lamé top"—pop right out of that little thing."

She felt the flush rising. The Jillian Joyner blush. The blush that didn't go with her Jammin' J.T. garb at all. She wondered why she'd never felt so exposed before—J.T. wasn't shy about this sort of thing.

"Don't follow me again, Russ." She turned, catching a glimpse of a couple staring in their direction. Of course. The two celebrities at war. In another two seconds, another couple would look to see what the others were staring at. Then another. And before long, half the room would have zeroed in on them.

She took a step away, but in a gesture that was growing frustratingly familiar, his hand snaked out to capture her. His fingers were firm at her waist, and before she could respond, he had moved up close behind her. The lapels of his jacket brushed against her bare back. She thought of the people who were watching. She thought of his body, lean and warm against hers. Her breasts ached.

"Then don't run away again."

She wanted to move out of his grasp, but something more than the grip of his fingers kept her still. An intensity that she seemed to breathe in through her skin kept her there, barely touching but pressed intimately against him.

"Why? Can you tell me why?" His voice was low, almost seductive, as he leaned close to her ear. His cheek grazed her hair and she felt a strand loosen. He reached for the strand, twirling it around a finger and brushing against her back, bringing her flesh alive as he did so. "What kind of game are you playing, Jillian?"

She closed her eyes, then opened them wide when she realized she had leaned ever so slightly into him. What was she doing, here in front of so many people? She swallowed, trying to alleviate the dryness in her mouth. "Can we talk about this some other time? I have to go."

He trailed a finger along the bare curve of her spine, stopping at her waist. "I'm warning you, Jillian. If you try to leave now, you'll be sorry. And all these people are going to love the show."

His taunting ultimatum gave her anger just the boost it needed to conquer the anxiety and the other, physical sensations that always threatened her equilibrium when Russ Flynn was around.

"All right, Russ." She turned in his arms to face him, pressing her breasts against his chest and telling herself the sensations coursing through her were the result of adrenaline. That was all. Pure, anger-produced adrenaline. She was onstage and she hoped every big shot in the room was getting an eyeful. She grinned up at him, sweetly venomous. "You want me. You've got me."

She snaked an arm up his chest, letting the fingers of one hand curl around the lapels of his dinner jacket. She inched the other hand higher, until her fingers toyed with the silver curls over his ear.

She was getting back at him. That's all. Just getting back at him.

He seemed momentarily stunned, as she swayed toward him. She smiled—the poutiest, most suggestive smile J.T. possessed. As she whispered, she brushed more closely against his lower body. The whisper came out even huskier than her best on-air teaser. "Whatsa matter, Russ? Don't know what to do with me now that you've got me?"

Suddenly the hands that had gone lax at her side tightened around her waist and she found herself pulled intimately against him.

"Big mistake, sweetness," he growled.

With one strong hand he locked her against his body. With the other, he roughly cupped her head and raised her lips to his. She opened her mouth to protest, but her stunned response was muffled as his mouth covered hers.

As it had been before, the meeting of their lips was savage in its intensity. His tongue probed her mouth and, after a moment of startled hesitation, she met it with her own. Hard and demanding, the kiss fed on their fury.

It was only when Jillian became conscious that her fingers were tugging at the buttons of his stiff dress-shirt that she realized Tallahassee's movers and shakers were enjoying the show.

She jerked away and stumbled backward, against the table. For a few seconds, all she could do was stare as his wild-eyed look changed to one of smug satisfaction. "That was nice, Jillian. But you needn't think you'll get off that easily."

Then he turned and strode off. Her heart still pounding, Jillian watched as Russ suavely moved among the guests, pausing to smile and shake hands. *As if nothing had happened.* Damn his effect on her! Jillian gripped the table behind her for support, trying to compose herself to work her way through the crowd. She had to get out. Call a cab. She took several deep breaths to calm herself. She felt a hand lightly tap her on the shoulder. Rosa had stepped up to the table.

"That was your best show yet," Rosa said sardonically as she pointed them toward the door.

Relieved Jillian followed her. "I don't want to hear any more about it, Rosa."

The first face she saw after they exited the ballroom was the reporter from the *Tallahassee Democrat*, standing by the pay phone in the foyer, fishing through her pockets.

Rosa pushed Jillian out the front door. "Something tells me your audience share after this little episode is about to increase dramatically."

RUSS RUBBED HIS ACHING head as he cued up the jingle that signaled the end of the traffic report. Finishing off that six-pack of beer he'd picked up on the way home from the Junior League gala the night before hadn't been the smartest move he'd ever made.

And it hadn't even saved him from staring into space half the night, wishing he'd simply thrown that two-faced Jillian over his shoulder and dragged her home with him to finish the little game she'd started—he'd started?—at the party.

He opened his mike and forced cheerfulness into his voice. "There you have it. Traffic's still a mess on Tennessee Street East, thanks to that apartment fire. So take your skateboards instead this morning, folks. You'll get there faster."

He fumbled with the carts, his fuzzy brain making it tough to pick out the final song of this morning's show. "Ten minutes from the top of the hour. Let's stick our nose in the newsroom, where Sharon will tell us a few secrets about the headlines coming up at nine. Sharon, what's new this morning?"

From the newsroom a few hundred feet down the hall, Sharon crisply outlined the top stories. "And, we'll have a report from the scene of that East Tennessee Street fire. Speaking of fires, Russ, I hear you were responsible for starting one yourself last night."

The postpromo banter between the news anchors and the DJ was obligatory, so Sharon's teasing comment shouldn't have taken him by surprise. But it did. Russ's lethargy was gone.

"Not this bad boy," he protested as good-naturedly as possible. "You must have some other firebug in mind."

"No, the word's out on this one, Russ. You were caught red-handed, fanning the flame. At least, that's the scoop in the morning paper."

Russ's hangover headache was pulverizing his brain. *Light,* he coached himself. *Keep it light.* "Oh, no! Not another case of mistaken identity. It's haunted me all my life, Sharon."

He stumbled through an agonizingly long minute of banter with Sharon, all the while cursing himself for failing to read the paper before going on air. Usually he read the paper. Except this morning, when he'd stumbled in on a few hours of fitful sleep and a hangover the size of FSU's Doak Campbell Stadium.

Music. He plugged in music, while his mind reeled at the memory of just how public he'd been with his display of . . . of what? Macho pique?

No, that wasn't what it had felt like at all. His anger had dissipated as soon as she'd thrown herself into his arms. Whatever kind of game Jillian Joyner—or Jammin' J.T. or whoever the hell she really was—had been playing, he had at least thrown her for a loop.

Actually, however, her game wasn't hard to figure. She had known who he was. Somehow, she'd had it in her mind to use his interest in her to bring him down in the ratings. That much was crystal clear. Why else would she have strung him along so callously all those weeks? No doubt laughing at him the whole time for chasing after her like a lovesick puppy.

He became livid just thinking about it. So livid he almost missed his cue that the country love-song was twanging its way to a close.

"That's it for another day, folks. Have a good one and I'll be back to help you survive another rush hour tomorrow morning. Until then, keep it on the road and don't start anything you can't finish."

Now, where did that come from?

Empty coffee mug hanging from his finger, Russ walked down the hall, calculating how long it would take him to refill his cup and produce the promos for tomorrow's show. With any luck, he could be home before lunchtime.

Just as he settled into the lumpy swivel chair in the production studio with a wickedly strong cup of black coffee, the door swung open and crashed against the wall. Flinching at the pounding in his head, Russ closed his eyes and waited.

"You'd better take your own advice, Mr. D.J."

It was Tony. Working-himself-into-an-ulcer Tony. Tony, who had chewed him out just about this time yesterday morning. Russ sighed and settled his aching head against the back of the chair.

"What's wrong now?"

"You've just started something you don't even want to think about finishing." Tony moved to the front of the room and tossed a crumpled section of the morning paper in Russ's lap. "Have you lost your mind?"

"Quite possibly." Russ tried to grin while he skimmed the paper in his lap. "If you've stumbled over a stray, it's highly likely—"

"What the hell do you mean running out and getting headlines for that damned woman?"

Sighing, Russ picked up the paper. At least there was no picture. He'd been afraid there might be a picture with some lurid caption: Country DJ Mauls Competition. But it was just a small item, in a small box beside the column about the Junior League gala. Radio Competition Heats Up the tiny headline said.

"Hell, Tony, that's so small nobody'll even notice."

"You'd better hope not, pal. I'm warning you, this woman is trouble. And you'd better not be responsible for any more publicity coming her way. Got it?"

"Sure, Tony. I get it."

Tony glared at him. "What in the world were you thinking, man? I know you like women, but this just wasn't smart. You know what I mean?"

"I wasn't— It was just— It was a joke. Okay? Just a joke. I figured I'd get her goat. Know what I mean?"

"A joke." Tony repeated the word incredulously. "Well, the joke's on you. And here's the punch line: Your job's on the line every day, Russ, and it ain't no joking matter."

After Tony left, Russ stared blindly at the control panel as if he'd never seen the equipment before.

Your job's on the line.

He was too burned-out for a ratings war and Tony probably knew that. The daily grind was no fun anymore. He couldn't even remember when he'd first grown weary of getting up at 4:00 a.m., weary of waiting with a knot in his gut for the ratings to come out every thirteen weeks, weary of listening while sponsors griped about the routine or skit that followed their spot. He didn't know when those things had eroded the high that used to come with performing. But they had.

And now that his career had become a battle-ground...

But what the hell else could he do? Become an office grunt like Tony? With no real education and no training in anything else, radio was his whole life. And had been for as long as he could remember. The first time he'd sat in front of a microphone, when he was still in high school, Russ had felt at home, comfortable. Where no one could see him, he'd been able to pretend that he was confident, witty, maybe even a little more sophisticated than the small-town listeners in Santiago, Florida.

Then, when he came to Tallahassee for college and got on WKIX, filling in during off-hours, he knew he'd found his place. He left college and threw himself full-time into savoring the confidence he drew from being on-air. As his career took off, the self-assurance he felt behind his mike had started to spill over into the rest of his life. From faking confidence, he had become confident.

At least, most of the time. At least until Lonnie had seen through his persona. Now Jillian had, as well.

And now, he might be finished in radio. And even though he'd come close lately to deciding he was fin-ished with it, it galled him to think he might not be the one to call it quits.

It especially galled him to think that the catalyst in his downfall might end up being a two-faced woman who had mesmerized him just as she had Tallahassee audi-ences.

IGNORING THE DOORBELL, Jillian pounded on the front door. She needed to pound on something, and the tiny red doorbell couldn't satisfy her urge to pound out her frustrations.

"What?" The door was flung open. His hand still on the doorknob, Russ looked as peeved as Jillian felt. "Oh, no. Not you."

The dread in his voice only heightened Jillian's aggravation. She stepped toward him, pointing a finger at his chest. "You started this, Mr. Flynn. So don't give me that look."

He backed away from her jabbing finger. "What look?"

"That 'What did I do to deserve this?' look." After shoving the front door shut, she stepped into the living room. "You started this mess and I'm here to make sure you end it."

"*I* started this mess?" Russ threw up his hands and stalked toward the couch. "If you had one honest bone in your body, none of this would have happened."

"This is not about honesty," she challenged, following him and grabbing an arm as he retreated. "This is about being one of those men who can't take no for an answer."

Russ whirled, bringing his face within inches of hers—so close she could see the flecks of violet in his eyes.

"You don't know anything about what kind of man I am! But I know all I need to know about the kind of woman who lies about—"

"I never lied about anything!" The fervor of her anger was growing now—she felt its heat surging through her.

Dropping her hand from his forearm, she struggled to suppress the inclination to back away from the threat of his closeness. "What I choose to tell a perfect stranger about my personal life is my business. And just because you feel compelled to chase anything that wears a skirt, don't go blaming me because I preferred to run."

"Blame you for running? I wouldn't dream of it. That seems to be what you do best, Ms. Joyner. What *do* your intimate friends call you, by the way?"

"When you fall into that category, Mr. Flynn, I'll make sure you get the answer." She was losing track of the reason she'd come here. "Listen, I didn't come here to attack you."

"No. You did that last night. In front of God and the press and everybody."

She flushed at his on-target accusation. "I just came here to tell you to leave me alone. I'm not interested in the kind of publicity you obviously use to stay on top and—"

"I don't believe this!" He leaned over, bringing his face level with hers. "You march in here like some self-righteous—after the way you—and you accuse me of—"

"You're sputtering, Mr. Flynn." The edge had gone out of her voice as she realized that Russ's vitriolic attack was growing weaker with every word. "A good jock never sputters."

"Damn you. I don't sputter." His words were an angry growl as he pulled her into his arms. "Dammit, woman."

At his touch, she was forced to acknowledge what she had refused to acknowledge before. She hadn't come to continue their running feud. She hadn't come to warn him off. She'd come for this: she'd come for his touch. And as she stared into his stormy blue eyes, she knew that he knew it, too.

She had no fight left in her after he pulled her close and covered her lips with his. His mouth crushed hers roughly against his and she parted her lips to accept his tongue.

With one hand, Russ possessively cupped her buttock, while he tugged at the hem of her sweater with the other, fighting his way up toward warm flesh. She arched into him, flattening her breasts against his chest.

Their legs tangled as Russ tried to bring them closer. Then he pushed Jillian over the arm of the couch, landing lightly on top of her. She spread her legs to draw him nearer. He sank down so that his hardness thrust against her. Raising her cotton sweater, he trailed his hand along her ribs until he touched the ripe fullness of her breasts.

"Please," she whispered, eyes closed. She was all sensation.

Russ lowered his head, pushed her sweater aside and covered a swollen nipple with his mouth. Then he unzipped her denim skirt. She felt his hand edging lower, beneath denim—and silk. Finally his fingers were tangling in her tight curls, seeking, moving lower, exposing her to his touch.

Exposing her.

She remembered, now, the warning that her body had been conveniently burying: This man was dangerous.

Just how dangerous she hadn't realized until this moment.

"No!" She grabbed his hand and pushed herself away from his touch, scurrying backward on the couch. Stumbling, she staggered to her feet. She pulled her sweater down and zipped up her skirt, all the while keeping a wary, fearful eye on him.

Russ groaned as he stared up at her, then lowered his face to the couch. "This isn't happening. Tell me this isn't happening."

"You're damn right it isn't happening." Jillian's voice was a breathless but determined gasp as she continued to back away from him.

Russ got up from the couch and took a step toward her.

"Don't try it, Russ. I warn you."

"And I'm warning you, lady. You'd better make up your mind what you're after. I won't ride this seesaw forever."

She heard the threat in his voice, but that wasn't what frightened her. What really struck terror was her realization that she wished he would act on that threat; wished he would toss her back down on the couch.

"I know what I'm after," she said recklessly. "And it isn't you."

Swearing under his breath, Russ moved toward her. "And what, pray tell, is it you're after?"

She had no response, and edged closer and closer to the door. Was her expression as wild as his?

"Tell me, Jillian. I want to know. What is it you're after?" If she allowed him to come near, she couldn't count on staying rational. "Is this some kind of scheme? Is that it? All part of the ratings game? Tell me, Jammin' J.T., what's going on in that scheming little mind of yours?"

"Yes." She grasped at the excuse he offered, certain it was the one thing that might keep him at a distance. "I'm out to bury you, Russ Flynn. Any way I can."

Taking advantage of his stunned silence, Jillian dashed to the front door. She ran all the way back to the safety of her condo.

6

JILLIAN WAS STILL quaking inside the next morning when she confronted her boss. Jim Towers was always formidable, but this morning Jillian felt as if all her reserves had been used in her confrontation with Russ the night before.

"I'm through with public appearances for a while." She mustered all the nonchalance she could. She sat back in the chair across from Towers, her arms draped casually, her legs lightly crossed, her voice composed.

But deep inside she still felt tumultuous.

"You are?"

Towers's calm response impressed her. Clearly, he had quickly learned that bullying his new star only made her more stubborn. She smiled. This wasn't going to be easy.

"That's right. We're running the risk of overexposure. There's enough interest out there right now to give us a good showing in the ratings."

"I'm not interested in a good showing when the ratings come out next month, J.T." He returned her smile. "I want progress toward the top."

"You'll get it."

"And you'll stick to the public-appearance schedule we set up when you arrived." He turned his attention back to the paperwork on his desk.

Irked by his dismissal, Jillian nevertheless knew it wouldn't do her cause any good to argue further right now. She stood and walked toward the door.

"By the way, J.T., I liked the stunt with Flynn." His voice halted her as her hand rested on the doorknob. "Outrageous. That's what people like about the Tallahassee Lassie. Keep her outrageous, J.T. And keep her in the public eye."

Jillian stewed over Towers's control over her as she pulled up scripts for a half-dozen ad spots she was slated to tape before she left for the day. With a phony smile and an even phonier lilt in her voice, she purred her way through a spot for a local restaurant. She pulled out all the stops on an ad for an office-furnishings company, which had been written with a couple of her characters in mind. She even played it straight on a special spot for the local chapter of the American Cancer Society.

And when she played the spots back, she realized none of them were any good. She was flat, flat, flat. Slumping back in her chair, Jillian listened to the tapes over and over again, waiting for them to get better.

It's all his fault, she told herself, glaring at a memo from Towers that was posted on the board above the equipment. He could have her creative or he could have her controlled, but he couldn't have her both ways.

Nobody calls the shots in Jillian Joyner's life, she told herself as she started retaping the spots, adding another on her appearance at FSU's annual student circus for good measure. *Nobody.*

But, as she left the station and climbed into her car, she knew just how ludicrous that claim was becoming. These days, it seemed, everyone but her had a say in how her life was to turn out; everyone—and especially Russ

Flynn, who had mastered her so completely that she actually relished the way he took command. In fact, her only regret was that he hadn't been a little more masterful when she had pushed him away.

"If only he'd made the decision you were too cowardly to make for yourself," she mumbled, chastising herself as she pulled into the condo parking lot.

The afternoon was quiet, but Jillian's mind was not. No matter what she tried to do, regrets about the night before haunted her. By late afternoon, she was stir-crazy.

When the doorbell rang, she was tempted to crawl behind the couch and pretend she wasn't home. After all, the only person who'd visited her since she'd moved to Tallahassee was the one person she needed to avoid at all costs.

She peered through the peephole. The dark head glancing around the complex wasn't the one she expected. But she wanted to avoid Rosa Miguel almost as much as she wanted to avoid Russ Flynn.

Then it hit her that once again, she was trying to shut people out of her life. She'd been doing it for so long—since she first left home for college. Now she was beginning to understand that she had simply swapped one trap for another. Had she run from so many people—was she still trying to run from so many people—that she risked having no personal life to protect?

Nobody ever said being a hermit would be fun, she grumbled to herself. She opened the door.

"You come bearing greetings from our old pal Towers, I presume." She smiled wryly at Rosa's reproachful look.

"Don't be coy with me." Rosa marched past Jillian without waiting for an invitation. "You get him all worked up, then blow the station and leave me to deal with him. Bad form, J.T. Really bad form."

Rosa laid her briefcase on the glass-topped dining table, stripped off her suit jacket and draped it carefully over the back of a chair, then faced Jillian. Her expression suddenly changed from accusing to confused.

"Say, what have you done to yourself?"

Involuntarily, Jillian reached up to touch the soft braid draped across her shoulder. She remembered now. No makeup. No funky clothes. No wild hair. Rosa was meeting the real Jillian Joyner for the first time. "Nothing. Just . . . I showered and . . ."

"Wow." Rosa circled her, mesmerized. "Let me take this in. You know, you don't even look like the same person."

"Really?"

"Really. I'll bet you could walk down the street and nobody would . . ." Her words tapered off.

Jillian turned away from the recognition in Rosa's piercing brown eyes.

"You didn't come here to talk about what a plain Jane I am." Jillian walked across the room to slouch into the corner of the overstuffed sofa. "You're here solely as a messenger from the Prince of Darkness. So, what gives?"

Rosa sat down in an armchair next to the couch.

"*You* tell me what gives. Towers said you've declared a moratorium on public appearances." While she spoke, Rosa loosened the top two buttons on her white silk blouse and rubbed the back of her neck. "He breathed fire when he said it. Making Towers crazy seems to be your favorite pastime."

"We've reached the saturation point." Jillian was so distracted by the transformation that was taking place in front of her that she forgot to sound forceful and convinced of her position. Rosa was now kicking off her shoes and pulling one foot up to rub her toes. It was the first time Jillian had seen her drop any of her rising-business-exec props. Now she knew why: Rosa Miguel without the armor didn't look especially intimidating; she looked friendly and pleasant and downright approachable. Which would never work in Towers's league, Jillian knew. "Um, anyway, we've reached the saturation point. Maybe it's time to pull back a little, build on the mystique."

"Horse hockey." Rosa smiled. "I'm the marketing guru here. You let me make those decisions."

"It's my life, Rosa. And I think it's time to cut back."

"What are you afraid of? Another little escapade like the one with Flynn?" When Jillian made no response, Rosa laughed softly. "Actually, I think Towers is right. It fits the persona. Maybe we could cook up something else...."

"Maybe you could tell Towers my show is good enough to stand on its own. I don't have to sleep with the public to get the ratings."

"J.T.—by the way, before I leave here today, I expect to know your real name—you know how to put on a good show. I know how to mold public opinion. You do your job and let me do mine. How about it?"

Jillian sighed. She hated it when she was wrong and somebody else was right. Especially when she really wanted to win. "I'm tired of all these public appearances. I want to stop. That's all."

"I'm not going to let you—"

The ringing of the telephone interrupted Rosa. Grateful for the reprieve, Jillian reached for the cordless phone at her elbow.

Audrey Tate's voice was breathless with agitation. "Jillie, how far are you from the airport, lovey?"

Jillian closed her eyes. "What difference could that possibly make?" But she already knew the answer.

"Should I rent a car and drive myself or just take a cab? I'm not going to have trouble finding your place, am I? Maybe the simplest thing would be to take a cab. What do you think?"

"I think you should stay where you are."

Audrey's laughter was breezy. Manufactured, but breezy. "Don't be silly. I don't have to remain in a loveless marriage."

"Mo— You're just upset. You and Henry love each other. Don't you think you should stay there and work things out?"

"I've tried that. For days. You wouldn't believe the demands he's making on me. So I'm leaving. And you know how the press is. They'll descend like vultures as soon as word gets out. I was thinking how peaceful Tallahassee would be. Just until the storm blows over. Wouldn't that be nice?"

Jillian could think of no effective counter argument. And besides, she wasn't prepared to launch a full-scale battle with her mother while Rosa sat with cocked ears just four feet away.

"I really don't think that's the best idea."

"Of course it is, Jillie. I've thought it all through. I'll be there tomorrow. I think it's tomorrow. Maybe the next. I don't remember, but the tickets are here somewhere," Audrey muttered to herself. Jillian could see her raking through piles of papers on her cluttered desk. "Oh, do you suppose you'll be on the air when I get there? I could ask the cabdriver to . . ."

Jillian listened, her dismay mounting. All her life, controversy and publicity had followed in Audrey Tate Joyner's wake. Every day of her childhood, Jillian had lived with the notoriety and the gossip and the uncomprehending stares of her schoolmates. And it had followed her after she'd left home, trailing her from college to college, from town to town, from job to job.

Why should it be any different now? she wondered, feeling the sting of tears in her eyes. *Get a grip, Jillie. You know she never could leave you in peace for long.*

"So I'll see you then, lovey." Audrey's voice was unspeakably cheerful as she hung up—so cheerful it gave Jillian a sharp pain right between the eyes.

"Problems?"

The voice brought Jillian back to wary attention. Rosa. *How much did I give away?* she wondered.

"Just something . . . personal."

"Tell me something personal, J.T."

"What do you mean?" The softening of Rosa's tone made her feel uncomfortable, even vulnerable. She didn't want to feel any more vulnerable than Audrey had already made her feel. She might lose it. Might lose it right here in front of Rosa.

She ignored the tiny voice inside her that insisted it would be perfectly okay to lose it—especially in front of Rosa.

"Look at me, J.T." The gentle command was more compelling than Rosa's typical toughness. Jillian looked up, and saw concern in her eyes. "I mean, tell me who you really are. It's obvious, seeing you here like this, that you're not the same person you are at the station. Who are you?"

Jillian tensed, hoping that her uneasiness wasn't apparent to Rosa. "This has nothing to do with what you came here to talk about."

"I doubt if you even know why I came here."

"Of course, I do. You came here because Towers is on your case. So now you're on my case. But it won't do any good, Rosa. My mind is made up."

Rosa shook her head. "Guess again."

"What?"

"Guess again. About why I'm here."

Jillian served her a blank stare.

"Because I like you." Rosa paused and fidgeted with the hem of her skirt—a gesture of uncharacteristic uncertainty. "You do your damnedest to keep anyone from liking you, but you slipped up and let me get too close. I like you and I'm worried about you."

Jillian didn't like the weak-kneed yearning to confide that took hold of her. "Worried? There's no reason to worry about me."

"Yes, there is. You're acting weird. And I want to know why."

"I'm not weird."

Rosa laughed. "Now, there's a matter for debate. Who was on the phone?"

"I don't have time for this."

"What's your real name?"

"That has nothing—"

"Why did you come here from Atlanta?"

"What is this, the Spanish—"

"Could be. Now tell me, who was on the phone?"

"My mother!" Jillian jumped up from the couch and paced across the room. Right now, she wished she were a drinking woman. "Okay? My mother. Now can we get off this kick?"

"What's wrong? She had some kind of bad news?"

"Nothing. Just . . . She's leaving her husband."

"I'm sorry."

A bitter laugh left Jillian's lips. "Actually, it's not a big deal. We've been through it plenty of times before."

"I see. How many times?"

Jillian shrugged. "Four. I think. Not counting my father."

Rosa whistled softly. "Now it's adding up."

"Your math is faulty, Miguel. You've reached a conclusion with only half the equation."

"So? What's the rest?"

Jillian clamped her mouth shut. She'd said too much already. What the hell had happened here? Didn't she remember who she was talking to? This was the woman whose job it was to generate publicity. This was the woman who could make her life miserable.

This was also the woman who said she'd come because she was worried.

Believe that, Jillian told herself, *and I'll show you some great swampland a few hundred miles south of here.*

But as she peered into Rosa's brown eyes, she found it hard not to believe.

Abruptly, Rosa stood and broke the silence. "Fine. I'll tell Towers you've come to your senses. The blitz is back on."

"No!" Jillian sank onto a pile of floor cushions, and clutched one of them to her chest. She struggled to keep the quiver out of her voice. "I've played that game all my life. I'm tired of it."

Rosa leaned closer. "What are you talking about?"

"I'm talking about growing up in the spotlight," Jillian said dully. "I'm talking about being Audrey Tate's daughter."

Rosa sank back into her seat. Her eyes widened and her mouth opened into an O of astonishment. "The comedian? The lady in the movies?"

"The lady in the movies. And *Time* magazine. And *People* magazine. And every supermarket tabloid that's ever been sold."

"Wow!"

Jillian smiled ruefully. "Wow. 'Wow' doesn't do it justice, Rosa. Trust me."

"No, you trust me. What's so bad about being Audrey Tate's daughter?"

"You mean what's so bad about playing out your whole life in the public eye? What's so bad about having the whole world know every time your mother runs off with another husband? What's so bad about living in a small town in Connecticut where the entire population knows when your mother starts sleeping with her director?" Jillian threw up her hands, past caring that her voice was cracking with emotion. "I don't know. Maybe it wasn't so bad, after all."

"Oh."

"And now she's coming here. And the vultures will be right behind her."

"But you're not a kid anymore, J.T. That kind of thing can't hurt you anymore."

"Rosa, I've spent the last half-dozen years building a quiet, private life for myself. Because I couldn't stand the thought of one more year under the microscope." She propped her chin on the edge of the pillow. "I haven't had three genuine friends since college. I've only dated men I could keep at a distance, men who didn't care if they ever found out what J.T. stood for. And if Audrey shows up here . . . Well, she doesn't know the meaning of quiet or private. If Audrey shows up here, we're talking a re-run of My Life: The Press Conference."

Rosa chuckled softly. "Towers would love it."

"Towers can take a long hike off a short pier."

"Listen, I can't work miracles." Rosa reached out to put a hand on Jillian's shoulder. "You've got a job to do and part of that job, right now, is meeting the public."

Jillian refused to beg. "Isn't there any other way?"

Rosa pursed her lips. "Dammit, J.T. You're putting me in a hot spot here. You know that, don't you?"

Hot spots were something Jillian understood. She nodded.

Rosa sighed loudly. "Then could you cut me some slack? I've got a job to do. And so do you."

The show must go on. Jillian understood that, too. As always, the show took priority over whatever pain she was feeling. "I know. You're right."

Rosa gave her shoulder a grateful squeeze. "I won't hang you out to dry. I'll do my best to keep Towers out of your hair. I'll shield your private life as much as I can. If Jammin' J.T. will continue to be her same crazy self out there, I'll do my best to see that—"

"Jillian. The name is Jillian."

"Nice to meet you, Jillian." Rosa smiled. "I'll do my best to see that Jillian has a nice, quiet life to come home to."

"You'd do that for me?"

"I'll do the best I can. Just so you understand—my best may not be good enough, especially if—"

"Especially if my mother sweeps into town with that notorious Audrey Tate flourish?"

"Especially then."

They sat and stared at each other. But as they stared, their shared gloom began to dissipate. And before they knew it, they were smiling, then laughing. They laughed until Jillian was dabbing tears from the corners of her eyes. For Jillian it was cathartic laughter that lifted her spirits—at least for the moment.

"Us Hispanic types make pretty good mother confessors, huh?" Rosa observed as their laughter died down.

"You're wasting your talents in the boardroom," Jillian remarked.

Rosa grimaced. "Tell me about it. You know, this is so bad I shouldn't even admit it. But all I really want to do is get married and have babies. A big brood. Now, how's that for living up to the stereotype?"

"Then, why don't you?"

"The last time I looked, making bambinos was not at the top in earnings potential." She propped her feet on the coffee table and slumped down in the chair. "And with a mother and a grandmother to support, I don't have much choice."

"Isn't there anyone else to help you?"

"What is this? Your turn as mother confessor?"

Jillian went into a self-protective mode. What was going on here? Was she really willing to risk accepting Rosa as her friend?

Or was the real question at this point, what choice did she have? The friendship was there, staring her in the face. Hers for the taking. If she had the courage.

She smiled, suppressing the fear that had ruled so much of her life. "Yeah. I think I'm ready for that."

Hours later, when they had consumed every diet soft drink in the condo and polished off two bags of potato chips, laughed some more, and confided, Jillian knew there was no way of returning to the isolation she'd condemned herself to in the past.

Jillian waved as Rosa pulled away from the curb. Strange how much more peaceful she felt, in spite of her unease at the prospect of revealing her real, off-air identity. In spite of Audrey's call. In spite of Towers's stubbornness. In spite of . . .

SHE HAD TO PUSH Russ Flynn out of her mind, as she jogged along the exercise trail that circled the complex. Sit-up stations and chinning bars were tucked into nooks along the path, but Jillian enjoyed it for its cool, fragrant canopy of oaks and flowering shrubs. She felt drawn into its peaceful depths.

Lost in thought, Jillian was unaware of the figure working his way across the parallel bars until she was beside the apparatus. So when he dropped down from the bars and almost into her path, she was startled. "Wh-what are you doing here?"

"I think that's pretty obvious," Russ barked. "The question is, what are you doing here? Looking for another place to hide? It's tough staying out in the open, isn't it, when you've got so much to hide?"

"That's not fair, Russ."

"Don't talk to me about fair, lady. I'm not the deceitful one."

Grabbing up the towel he'd left on the ground beside the parallel bars, Russ abruptly turned and jogged away.

Jillian's feeling of serenity vanished. Russ was still angry. Very angry. Angry enough to make her life miserable, if he chose to. And why shouldn't he? Hadn't she provoked him? Hadn't she brought it upon herself?

7

JILLIAN GRIMACED AT THE final words of the syrupy love song. *Bah, humbug!* she thought, switching her sour expression for a big smile as she opened her mike again.

"Ah, love," she whispered to her listeners. "Who's in love out there? Come on, 'fess up. You're in love. I can see it in your eyes. Give me a call and tell me how you met your sweet'ums. I've got dinner for two for the lover with the best story."

The phone lines lit up before she even finished giving the number over the air. Was it the free dinner, she wondered skeptically, or was it really love that fired them up?

She read an ad for the restaurant giving away the free dinners, then grabbed the first of the flashing lines.

"This is Jammin' J.T., your Tallahassee Lassie." She knew her smiling voice was perfect, despite the cynicism lurking in her heart. Jillian Joyner, consummate actor, trained at her mother's knee. "You're on the air, so keep it clean. What's your love story?"

Some were sweet, some were funny, some pushed the limits of innuendo—just the kind of thing listeners loved, J.T. knew. After her few short weeks in Tallahassee, whenever J.T. asked the listeners to call, the switchboard lit up like fireworks. The response was satisfying, but right now Jillian was weary of thinking about, talking about, laughing about love.

"What's your love story?" she asked for the tenth time.

"I think *you* deserve the dinner for two," teased the voice of a young woman on the other end.

Jillian laughed, hoping the sound wasn't as hollow as it felt. "Not this kid. The Tallahassee Lassie doesn't have time for jammin' *and* lovin'. And if one's got to go, you can guess which one it is."

"But I hear you had a pretty romantic meeting yourself this week." The voice grew wistful. "Please, J.T., tell us about it. We just love you. And Russ Flynn is the ultimate. We think what happened is so romantic. We're dying to hear all about it."

Jillian's mouth went dry. The control room seemed to fade away. All she could think of was Russ Flynn and her runaway emotions—because what was plaguing her was more than lust. When she'd knocked on Russ's door two afternoons before—in a split second of self-discovery before he opened the door—she knew she missed being around him. She missed sparring with him. She missed the teasing "Gotcha!" in his blue eyes when he bested her. She missed the pleasure of finally knowing a man who wasn't intimidated by her sharp tongue.

Russ Flynn meant more to her than kisses she couldn't resist. She *liked* him. Genuinely. And that, she recognized instantly, was even more frightening than just liking the way he filled out a pair of jeans.

She drew a deep breath and reminded herself that even a few seconds of dead air was death on the radio.

"I was hoping somebody would ask about that. I thought that guy at the other station—what's his name? I never can remember his name—and I pulled it off pretty well. I hate to disappoint you, but what happened the other night was . . . That is, sometimes in this business you . . ." She couldn't say it. The words *publicity stunt* wouldn't be forced past her lips. "It was just a joke. That's all. Just a joke."

A bad joke. And the joke's on me. Because, no matter how she struggled to rationalize away her feelings, they couldn't be denied. She wanted Russ Flynn. He wanted her. But it would never be—not if she could keep her wits about her and the repercussions in sight.

"A joke?" The woman sounded as unconvinced as Jillian's own subconscious. "It didn't look much like a joke."

"Of course, it didn't look like a joke. We're trained professionals." Her quip sounded fatuous even to her own ears. "Able to pull off even the most difficult stunts with ease. So don't be fooled. And don't try it at home. Remember, we're trained professionals."

"You mean you can kiss like that and—"

Jillian interrupted with a laugh. "You call that a kiss? Now, that is a joke. We're running into the news, Tallahassee, so let's award that dinner for two to the couple who met at last year's FSU circus."

She triggered a cassette that held the sound of wild applause and whistles, passing a hand over her forehead as the last caller hung up.

"And speaking of the FSU circus, the big event is this week, folks. I'll be there, giving away Tallahassee Lassie visors to the first two hundred people who come by the WFLA booth. So, come on down. Who knows? You may meet your true love, like Donnie over at the Department of Natural Resources."

Or you may, she thought to herself as she started the lead-in to the news, *make a perfect clown of yourself. Like this kid just did.*

She barely got out of the control room without throttling Bruce, who wanted to rehash the final telephone conversation. And before she could lock herself in the studio where she planned to work on her promos for her live broadcast from the FSU circus, Rosa slipped in, and leaned against the doorjamb wearing a smug grin.

"I thought you'd rather see me than Towers."

"Gracious, yes. I'm thrilled." Jillian knew she sounded grumpy. She felt grumpy. She wanted to be grumpy. Maybe if she was grumpy enough, everybody would just leave her alone.

"And in such a sweet mood this morning. Your love life must really be taking off."

The notepad Jillian picked up from the control panel and pitched toward Rosa's head missed its mark by half a foot. "My love life is—"

"In the public domain?"

"Off-limits."

"Apparently not. I hear the listeners are wild to know more. And I can't believe I let you get away without spilling your little secrets last night."

"The next person who brings up my love life will find hungry alligators in the front seat of her BMW after work one day."

"But if it's just a joke?"

"Did you talk to Towers about my public appearances?"

"Not before he got to me about your love life."

Jillian groaned.

"He liked the call this morning. Really thinks we ought to do more to play that up. It's obvious, he said, that this morning's caller is a 'KIX listener. Also obvious she was listening to you instead. So he's thinking of playing Cupid."

"Tell him to put away his bow and arrow."

"I told him we'd work on it."

"You what? You're going soft in the head. Do you know that? After all I told you, do you think for one minute that I'd—"

Rosa walked over, clamped a hand over Jillian's mouth and pushed her down into a chair. "I told him we'd work on it. And if we're lucky, he'll forget about it. But digging in and telling him no is like waving a red flag in front of a bull's nose. He'll be ready to charge. And then where will you be?"

Jillian slumped in the chair and Rosa removed her hand.

"Packing my gear."

"Exactly. So, play this thing cool and let me handle it. Think you can manage that?"

"I'll try."

"Good girl." Rosa paused at the door and gave Jillian one final smug grin. "By the way, it didn't look much like a joke to me, either."

"LEARN TO LOVE IT," Jillian mumbled between breaths, as she jogged along the exercise trail, her heart pumping furiously and her calf muscles screaming at the abuse. Driven by excess energy, Jillian had chosen tonight to begin the intensive aerobic exercise program she'd put off for months. Between this morning's call, the run-in with Rosa and being on red-alert for her mother's arrival at any moment, she was totally wired up. Every little while, she'd looked out the sliding-glass doors from her bedroom to the pool. It had been empty. She'd rearranged the books on her shelves. The pool was still empty. She'd cleaned out the refrigerator. By now, dusk was settling in and the pool was still empty. So she'd written letters to the few friends she'd left behind in Atlanta.

But when she'd caught herself, scrub brush in hand, heading for the bathroom, she knew she'd gone too far. So she'd gone to the exercise trail, instead. The two-mile jog had eaten up her excess physical energy. But her mind was still in restless turmoil.

Then, spotting a familiar form walking toward the spa, she finally acknowledged that she'd been waiting for Russ to appear.

And now that she'd seen him, she had to see him close up. Knew she had to talk to him. Knew that she wanted to set things right.

She rushed back to her condo. If Russ was headed for the hot tub, she would join him. Cornered there, he'd have to listen. And she'd have to keep from losing her head. She'd be cool. She would talk to him rationally, she told herself, as she put on her swimsuit. Then, they could shake hands and go back to . . .

Back to what? she wondered as she draped a towel over her shoulders and went toward the spa. Back to being friendly competitors? They'd never been that. What had they been, before Russ had discovered the secret she'd been keeping?

A man and a woman playing the game of discovery. That's what they'd been.

Her certain step faltered at the thought.

She straightened her back and kept walking. *Never mind that*, she coached herself. She had to resolve this. It was eating her up. It was ruling her life. It was . . .

She melted against the door at the sight of him, lolling back in the tub, steam dampening the tight dark curls on his tanned chest. His eyes were closed, the hair at his temples also dark and damp. Jillian's mouth went dry.

Not such a good idea, after all!

But she closed the door behind her anyway. And, as an afterthought, turned the lock. To give them privacy. So they could talk, she told herself.

Ri-i-i-ight, taunted the soul of Jammin' J.T., which was lusting after the hard, lean body lolling in the tub, even as Jillian's timidity fought to run from this particular time slot.

He looked up when the lock clicked into place. His expression hardened when he saw her; his shoulders squared and he seemed to squeeze closer against the side of the tub.

"What are you doing here?"

She dropped her towel to the wooden floor and sat down on the edge. Dipping her feet and legs into the steaming water, she felt what little fight she possessed drain away. "Looking for you," she admitted.

"Ready for another cat fight?"

She ignored the animosity in his voice.

"I'm ready to make up." She saw no reaction in his face. "Or at least call a truce."

His eyes searched hers and she prayed he would see whatever it would take to make him believe her. She thought she saw a softening in his gaze before he looked away.

"Why?"

"Because I don't like this...this anger that's grown up between us." She wanted to move closer to him, but she needed a sign first. "I thought we were friends, and ..."

There was no sign, but in a matter of seconds they were far closer than she'd had in mind. In a flash, Russ had maneuvered himself in front of her. His long, strong hands reached up and pinned her shoulders down, pulling her into the tub. Despite the sharp ceramic edge at her back as she slid downward, she was aware only of his hands on her shoulders, his damp, hot skin against her damp, hot skin.

"You thought we were friends?" His words were harsh, but his voice was quiet and controlled. "Friends don't lie to each other, Jillian. Did that ever occur to you?"

"I never lied."

"You never told the truth. Isn't that the same thing?"

Her legs drifted against his in the water. His were slick and hard and long. When she didn't answer right away, he leaned closer. Their thighs pressed together. The heat against her belly increased and she knew he was close— as close as she'd wanted, as close as she'd feared.

"Isn't it the same thing, Jillian? You were deceiving me. Didn't that ever bother you?"

"I didn't . . . I wouldn't . . ." But she couldn't find the right words to form her protest. Her mind was preoccupied with sensation. Without thinking, she felt her legs tangle with his. Had she done that? She couldn't be sure.

Russ closed his eyes. When he spoke, his voice had lost all its harshness. "Well, it bothered the hell out of me."

"I'm sorry." The words floated out, as wispy as the steam swirling around their bodies. She reached up to touch his face, willing the tightness around his eyes to relax.

"Are you?" He pressed against her hand, like a cat stretching to deepen the stroke against its fur. Jillian obliged, curving her palm to his face, easing her fingers back into his damp hair. She pulled him closer, or he moved closer—she wasn't sure which. "I'm sorry, too."

His mouth hovered over hers, then covered it. His lips were full and soft and coaxing, slick with moisture. Hers slid against them and opened in invitation. When he obliged, she knew she wanted more.

Her fingers sought his hard, slick back and she felt his muscles quiver as her hands roamed lower and lower.

"This isn't enough," he murmured, pulling away and looking into her eyes.

His hands grasped the straps of her suit and slipped them down, baring her to the waist. He didn't touch her, simply pulled back enough to caress her with his eyes. The ache in her nipples—already tight—increased under the intensity of his gaze.

At last, he brushed a finger over one breast, and she groaned as he lowered his mouth to the aroused tip. His tongue swirled over it, then he sucked it gently between his lips. Her groan deepened and she arched into him.

While he buried himself between her breasts, she tugged at his trunks, lowering them over his buttocks. He was hard, smooth and strong beneath her seeking fingers. She dug into him, pulling him more tightly against her. Sheathed in warm water, his erection slipped between her legs and she tightened her thighs to hold him there. He moved against her, continuing to nuzzle her breasts until she could stand the teasing no longer.

In one swift movement, she slipped out of his arms and shed her swimsuit, letting it drift away on the water. "Now," she said softly. "Now, nothing else is hidden."

"Nothing?" He reached out but didn't pull her to him. Instead, his hand slipped between her thighs, cupping her mound.

She could barely speak as a persistent finger played against her, coaxing her to submission. She mouthed an answer, knowing the only sound she could make would be a gasp or a sigh.

Feeling herself tighten in response to his tender manipulation, she arched forward, and encircled his swollen shaft with her hand. Slowly she stroked upward, to the tip, then back. Slowly. As slowly but as certainly as the tension was building to the breaking point inside her.

She guided him toward her, but he held her back. "Not yet, Jillian. Not yet." His whisper was soft, but the movements of his hand grew more insistent as he spoke. "I want to watch you. I want to see your face when you lose control."

"But . . ."

The protest was futile. Watching him watch her, feeling his penis erect in her hand as her breath quickened and the movement of her hips intensified, she had no choice but to grant his wish. Her climax washed over her in waves of sensation that made her cry out as she arched back in the water.

She floated, with his free hand supporting her back while his other hand gradually slowed and pulled away. Then she felt him part her legs. The swollen shaft she had held in her hand nudged at flesh still quivering with sensation. She was whimpering, but couldn't stop the helpless sound—couldn't stop any part of the complete surrender he had wanted.

"Please," she whispered as he hesitated, her aching flesh straining against his.

"Are you sure?"

In answer, she wrapped her legs around his hips and pulled him close, drawing his flesh into her as she did so. As they joined, the waves started again, drowning her, shattering her.

Then he moved inside her, holding her buttocks in his hands and rocking her against him—smooth skin against smooth skin—until she felt him tighten and swell and explode inside her, again and again.

Finally, their bodies stilled. Her cries of pleasure subsided. She leaned into him, cradling her head against his shoulder. He whispered her name and the sound brought a smile to her lips. With her eyes closed, their bodies still joined, she snuggled closer.

This was right. She felt it. Knew it. Why it was so, she wasn't certain. It was a peace she hadn't known since . . . She couldn't remember when—if ever.

"Come home with me." His whisper was muffled as he nibbled at her earlobe. She shivered at the touch of his lips and teeth. But her half smile started to fade. What had he said? "Stay with me tonight."

She was barely aware that she had stiffened in his arms and pulled away to unlink their bodies. "I can't."

He looked into her eyes, beguiling her. She lowered her gaze. "It's better not to. I have to be up so early."

Gently lowering her, he tilted her chin up so their eyes met again. He was smiling. "I know. So do I."

Now her smile faded completely. Of course, he did. And she remembered now why the tranquillity she felt was so incongruous.

My goodness! Wouldn't Towers be pleased with this little development.

Apprehension destroyed her sense of peacefulness.

"What's wrong, Jillian?" he asked with concern.

She backed away. Her swimsuit floated against her elbow and she grabbed it, yanking it guiltily in front of her. "This was a mistake."

"A mistake? How the hell can you call what just happened a mistake?"

"Russ, don't you see? You're...who you are. And I'm...who I am."

"And who is that, Jillian? Just who the hell are you?" In one swift motion, he was out of the tub, standing over her, swim trunks in one hand, water running in rivulets down his long, lean body. The sight of him renewed the desire that had scarcely been quenched by their lovemaking. "Are you a voice? A personality? A whore to the ratings? Or are you the woman who just made love with me?"

Even while she registered his fury, she felt her body tighten with longing. And saw his body begin to betray him with a passion that obviously his fury couldn't deny.

But she had to remain rational. One of them had to. "All those things exist, Russ, whether we like it or not. A part of us does belong to the station, whether we—"

"I like the part of you that belonged to me for a few minutes a lot better than whatever part belongs to WFLA," he bit back, leaning over to step into his trunks. "I may not be a brain with a college education, but I'm smart enough to realize we obviously play by different rules. Thanks for the quickie, J.T."

And he was gone, leaving her adrift in water that now felt cold against her bare skin.

8

WITH A BIG SMILE and a wink, Jillian passed out what must have been the three-jillionth I Love My Tallahassee Lassie sun visor of the day.

"These are hotter than the circus memorabilia," Rosa gloated, pointing across the lot that bordered Pensacola Street to the yellow tent where FSU circus T-shirts and caps were on sale. "I told you these neon colors were just the ticket."

"They give me a headache." *Not entirely true*, Jillian conceded to her guilty conscience. The headache wasn't the fault of the eye-offending neon hues of the cheap plastic visors. The splitting headache was an irritating mishmash of Jim Towers and Russ Flynn and a certain redheaded comedian who could burst into town any minute.

But even the prospect of another grand entrance by Audrey Tate Joyner was minor in comparison to other, more immediate worries.

"Here comes another wave." Rosa nodded toward a group of students making a beeline for the WFLA booth, which had been a focal point for much attention all afternoon. "Smile. Be witty."

She smiled. She was witty. At least, she hoped she was witty. She seemed to be handling the witty part okay—everyone had been smiling back, laughing at all the right places.

But for Jillian, the adrenaline that had got her through her morning show had long since peaked and was now plummeting to a dangerous low. When she'd been on the air, it had been easier to perform, to forget Jillian's problems and lose herself in J.T. But now, without the microphone as a buffer, it was harder. And the harder it became not to think about Russ Flynn.

No. Not to think about Russ. He wasn't so much filling her head with thoughts as he was filling her with emotions. With anguish. With fear. With dread. With anticipation. And with sensations that hadn't stopped pulsing through her all night long, as she'd tossed and turned.

She couldn't believe what she'd said and done.

She couldn't believe he'd walked away.

She couldn't believe how fervently she'd prayed he hadn't walked away forever.

Forget Jillian, she coached herself, flashing a wide, inviting smile at two young men eyeing her almost timidly from the middle of the parking lot near Doak Campbell Stadium. *Let J.T. ride this afternoon.*

"What time's the next remote?" she asked Rosa, hoping she would be back on the air soon.

Rosa checked her watch. "About ten minutes. Got anything in mind? I could get one of the FSU officials to give us some hype about the circus. Aren't they touring the Bahamas this year?"

"I'll find something." She breathed a sigh of relief. Ten minutes until airtime. She glanced around, hoping that someone would show up who'd be good on radio. These remotes were great if you chanced upon people in the crowd who didn't freeze up when you shoved a mike in their face.

Her eyes alighted on the two teens who'd been hanging back, giving her a careful once-over from a safe distance. She smiled again, enticingly, and crooked a finger at them. They didn't fit in this crowd, she could tell that. They weren't easygoing, smooth-operating college kids; they seemed poor and unsure of themselves, and not quite slick enough to cover that fact very convincingly.

Jillian had never been poor. But the unsure and unconvincing part, she certainly could empathize with. She picked up two of the sun visors and held them out.

"These have your names on them." She smiled—a flirty little smile that seldom failed, even with adolescents. It didn't fail now, either. Grinning shyly, the two walked toward her.

Youth Power, their faded T-shirts said. But she didn't recall that Tallahassee had a problem with youth gangs; and even if it did, these two didn't look like trouble. They looked like good kids who knew a lot about bad times. She reached out and clamped the visors on the two young heads, one of them covered with short, dark curls and the other with lighter, wavy hair.

"I thought so. Perfect." They thanked her shyly. "So, what's this Youth Power business? Can I join?"

They laughed and the tall black youth jabbed the other in the arm, his smile revealing a chipped tooth. "No, lady. Just us dumb kids."

"We're not dumb." The voice was soft and shy, but his eyes flared with protest.

She grinned at them, and their timid smiles grew more open.

"I'm Jammin' J.T. from WFLA and we're going to be on the air in a few minutes." She leaned a hip against the table in the booth. "Would you like to tell the station's listeners about Youth Power?"

The soft-spoken youth reached up to twist the chip of crystal in his pierced ear. "You mean, be on the radio?"

"Sure. If you'd like." She smiled at his friend. "If you swear you'll keep a leash on your language."

"Wow! That'd be cool. My name's Howie and my mom's been listening to you."

Jillian felt her heart soften at the vulnerability she picked up on at the mention of his mother. There were, she supposed, all kinds of problems to complicate childhood and all kinds of mothers to complicate the complications.

"Two minutes," Rosa cautioned. "Are you sure..."

"I'm sure." Jillian began to hook up the equipment that would enable her to converse with the afternoon DJ at WFLA while she gave Howie a mock stern look. "And what do you mean, your mom listens to me? What's your problem? Why aren't *you* listening? You can't listen to rap all day."

His eyes brightened again at her teasing. "No, ma'am. But sometimes I listen to—"

"He listens to me."

Jillian almost choked. The voice at her side wasn't familiar only to the two teens in front of her. It was a voice she knew far too intimately herself. Cranking her public persona up to full strength, she turned to him with the same dazzling smile she used for all her fans.

The smile fizzled only slightly in the face of his own cool smile. But what had she expected? The puppy-dog friendliness that she had no doubt abused to the breaking point?

"Listens to you, does he?" *The show must go on*, she coached herself. "I knew you must still have a listener out there somewhere, Flynn."

"A few," he conceded. His tone was glacial, his eyes icier. "I'd have a few more, I suppose, if I were willing to go to the lengths some people are."

Something inside Jillian shriveled and died.

"I wouldn't sweat it," she said brightly. Too brightly? She couldn't be sure. "Wit, charm and intelligence can't be forced."

"What else, J.T.? Are there any other things you can't force? Or can you create all the rest of it out of thin air, too?"

"Sure. If you've got the talent."

"And the stomach for it."

"Hey, Russ, you didn't tell us you knew Jammin' J.T."

For the first time, Jillian noticed that three other young men hovered at Russ's side. They, too, wore Youth Power T-shirts.

"Yeah, dude. You been holding out on us. Why didn't you tell us you knew Jammin' J.T.?"

"Because I don't, guys. Not really."

"But enough to introduce us, huh, dude?"

"See, Russ is one of our, like, sponsors," the teenager with the chipped tooth explained to Jillian. "He shoots baskets with us after school. And he yells at us when we don't study enough. And . . ."

"Wait a minute," Russ protested. "I don't yell at you."

The five teenagers all howled their disagreement. "Sure you do, dude. You're on us like ugly on a pig."

While the others argued good-naturedly, Howie leaned close to Jillian and whispered, "He helped me with my math. I'd have flunked for sure if he hadn't stayed on my case. That's the first C I ever made in math."

"You sound kind of proud of it."

He grinned. "Yeah. Just a little. My mom . . ." He hesitated. "Mom was proud, too. I know she was."

Rosa tapped Jillian on the shoulder. "The producer's got the station on the phone. Ready?"

Jillian glanced back at Russ, then over at the teens' hopeful faces. "Sure, why not?"

After a few seconds of small talk with the afternoon DJ, Jillian launched into some background on the circus.

"FSU may be best known for the way the Seminoles hustle up a first down on the football field," Jillian said. "But when FSU went coed in 1947, school officials wanted to find a sport that men and women students could study together. And the FSU circus was born.

"For the next two weekends, thousands will pour into the yellow tent on Pensacola Street to see students who have learned to walk the high wire and survive the flying trapeze." Jillian then moved on to questions about Youth Power.

"And I understand you get some pretty high-powered help with your math, Howie."

"Yeah. Russ Flynn helped me out. He's better at algebra than he is shooting hoops, and that's the truth."

"So that's what you do when you aren't making bad jokes on the radio." Jillian thrust the mike in Russ's direction. "You're resident math pro at the Youth Center off Tennessee Street."

He put his hand over the mike to steady it, capturing her hand under his. "I guess you could say I know what adds up and what doesn't."

Jillian frowned, but kept her voice impersonally cheerful. "And why so interested in this project?"

"DJs do a lot of things just for publicity," Russ said pointedly, his fingers tightening on the mike—over her hand. Suddenly she felt the humidity in the air. Her palm grew damp. Her breathing grew heavy. "You know what I mean, J.T. What's going to boost the ratings, put me in the public eye? You do know what I mean, don't you, J.T.?"

"I know what you mean." A pulsing started in her hand, resisting the hand that stayed with her as they shared the mike. *And I know what you're getting at, too*, she warned him with a look.

"But this isn't one of those projects. I like these kids. They matter to me—a lot. I wouldn't give myself to them if they didn't." His eyes bored into hers. "I know some people won't understand that. But it's true."

Unable to stand the closeness, his touch, any longer, Jillian smiled and dismissed him, turning back to the young people for a few more comments before she signed off.

"That's all from the campus for now. Catch you next hour?"

"Right, J.T. And we'll keep the news team on alert in case you and your fellow morning man declare war out there." The afternoon DJ laughed in her ear. "You're not planning to shoot him out of a cannon or anything, are you?"

"No. But if you've got a whip and chair, I could beat him back to that other station and get a citation from the student body at the same time," she quipped, marveling at how lighthearted she sounded and how heavyhearted she felt.

It was over. The connection was broken, listeners were no longer on the other end. And Jillian felt every bit of energy zap out of her body.

"Thanks, Flynn," she said tightly.

"Anytime you need pumping up."

He wheeled and was gone, his young entourage following him toward the tent where the circus was about to get under way.

Would this afternoon ever end? Jillian looked pleadingly at Rosa. "How much longer?"

"Good question," Rosa said dryly. "Soon, I'd say. I don't think you can take much more."

WHAT WAS GOING ON TODAY? Wherever Russ showed up, there was commotion. First, there was the near brawl when he'd insisted that André, Howie and several other boys from the Youth Center accompany him to the circus at FSU.

"No way, man," André had insisted stubbornly. "I ain't going over there with a bunch of uppity college kids."

But Russ had been determined to expose them to a college campus—and in doing so, demonstrate that they could fit in and be comfortable there. He remembered all too well just how nervous he'd been about setting foot on campus for the first time. "What are you afraid of?"

No more persuasion had been necessary. Cowardice was not an accusation to be taken lightly, and the fourteen-year-old was just brazen enough to prove Russ wrong—no matter how right he'd been.

That had been the first commotion. Next, there had been the testy little scene with Jillian. Or J.T. Or whoever the hell she was. Then, the madhouse of the circus—an annual affair that spotlighted the newly acquired skills of FSU circus students. An entertaining commotion, but a commotion nevertheless.

But he'd never seen a one-woman commotion, he thought as he secured his motorcycle, until now.

The woman was standing in the middle of the courtyard at his condo. A wide-brimmed red hat hung from a yellow sash around her neck, leaving a headful of orange-red curls glistening in the sun. Her plump but firm curves were encased in a swimsuit the color of a fire engine, which was covered by a gauzy turquoise thing that flowed down to her yellow high-heeled sandals.

She looked familiar and she was waving a cellular phone at someone on an upstairs balcony.

"What's a little nudity, he wants to know!" Her voice was loud and outraged. "Easy for him. He's never had a nip or a tuck in his life. I'd have to remodel the whole damned thing to get ready for a nude scene. And you should see the hard young hunk they want me stripping down to my cellulite with. No nudity, no deal, he says. Easy for him."

He recognized her as soon as she opened her mouth. Audrey Tate. *The* Audrey Tate—probably America's best known, most-loved, most outrageous comic actress for at least thirty years, the daughter of a stand-up comedian who had started in vaudeville before storming Hollywood. If he remembered correctly, she had started out as a child radio star in the forties, then starred in a series of romantic comedies in the fifties. Her famous trademarks were fire-engine-red hair and the best comic wit and timing in the business.

And now, she was standing right here in front of him, raising the throaty-sweet voice that no one in America could mistake.

"So, tell him no," came another voice. A voice that Russ couldn't mistake.

"Tell him no?" Audrey's voice jumped up another octave. "And never work again? It's an Oscar-caliber part, he says. How can I say no?"

Russ took three more steps to round the corner and follow the actress's gaze, although he didn't need to see to confirm what he already knew. Staring down at the actress, who was now furiously punching buttons on the cellular phone, was Jillian.

Jillian, her auburn waves glinting back a softer gold than the brass of Audrey Tate's wild mane. Jillian, her curves not quite as generous. Jillian, her voice not quite as theatrical and piercing. But there was no mistaking its similarity.

If Las Vegas had been taking bets that these two weren't mother and daughter, Russ knew he would have staked the family farm against the odds.

Suddenly, a lot of things added up. And he knew he couldn't keep his mouth shut.

"I say take the part."

Two pairs of green eyes—one pair pleasantly intrigued, the other pair guardedly suspicious—glanced in his direction. He smiled—his best boyish smile—directly at Audrey Tate.

To hell with the daughter, he thought, without admitting to himself that he might be goading the mother just to needle the daughter.

"Who asked you?" demanded Jillian from the balcony.

And right on its tail, a coy comment from Audrey. "Oh, you *would* say that, young man. I suppose you've been dying to see me *au naturel* for years."

He took a step closer to the legendary performer. Yes, it all added up now. Jillian's flair for comedy and her thirst for ratings. She was headed somewhere. Headed somewhere he could never follow, even had he been so inclined. No wonder he mattered so little to her. He was just a minor obstacle. Something to be stepped over. Or on.

But, if it all added up so neatly, why did the answer leave him feeling so sick?

He did what any pro would do under the circumstances. He upped the charm. With the disarming smile that had worked such wonders with all the women he'd ever known—except one—he took the phone from Audrey Tate and draped an arm around her slender shoulders.

"I'd be lying if I didn't admit that the thought of a Tate woman in the altogether wasn't tantalizing," he said with a teasing wink.

She smiled up at him with a sly look in her eye that told him she was much more astute than the public image she had created and polished over the years. She glanced toward Jillian, then back at him, modestly lowering thick lashes over her eyes.

"I don't doubt that for a minute, young man."

His laugh was cut off by the brusque voice from the balcony. "Can we finish this discussion in the privacy of my living room?"

Knowing the invitation was meant for only one of them, Russ chose to misunderstand. Gesturing with the hand that held the cellular phone, he questioned Audrey. "Do you suppose she's serving refreshments?"

Audrey shook her head. "I think not. So stuffy, you know. You do know, don't you?"

"Stuffy?" He looked up at Jillian, impatiently tapping her foot on the indoor-outdoor carpet of her balcony. "Mmm, on occasion, at least. Not always. But certainly on occasion."

Audrey raised an eyebrow. "Is that right, Jillie? Not always stuffy? Gracious, I'm glad to hear that." She linked arms with Russ and leaned her ample bosom against him. "Tell me more. For starters, tell me your name."

"Russ!" Jillian's angry tone commanded his attention. "Would you please leave us alone? And, Mo—Audrey, would you please come in the house so we can discuss this like civilized people."

Shrugging, Audrey disengaged her arm from his with what was clearly exaggerated reluctance. With a feline smile, she began to back away from Russ. "See what I mean? So stuffy."

Russ smiled. So much alike, these two. And so different. Almost as if Jillian had created one self to follow in her mother's footsteps. And another to follow as divergent a path as possible.

He returned Audrey's playful shrug. "I think I've been dismissed. You'll have to do your best."

"Oh, dear. And I've been such a failure up until now." She smiled and retrieved the phone. "I was so hoping for a little help this time."

Then she scampered back toward the condo. "I'm coming, lovey, I'm coming. Calm yourself. It really isn't as bad as it seems. Perhaps he's right. Perhaps I should take the part. That's what I told your father. If only he hadn't been so bullheaded."

While Audrey chattered all the way to the door, Russ's gaze was drawn to the balcony. But Jillian had already gone back into hiding.

At least now he knew what he was up against. A third-generation comedian with her sights set on the stars. And on her way to the big time, she could easily wipe out his modest career. Her legendary background could sky-rocket her to the top of the ratings, leaving him in the black hole. And, no doubt, out of a job.

If that's the game Jillian Joyner chose to play, Russ knew now it was no contest. The ratings battle was over before he could strike a single blow.

JILLIAN HELD A COOL washcloth to her forehead. It didn't help the headache she'd been nursing all day. And it certainly wasn't helping block out the look on Russ's face when he'd recognized Audrey.

"Poor lovey." Audrey's delicate perfume wafted nearby. Jillian felt a peck of a kiss land lightly on top of her head and heard just the right inflection of motherly concern in the voice. "What can I do to help with your headache?"

A faint smile crossed Jillian's lips. *Go home.* "It'll be fine, Mother."

"What a nice young man. You've been holding out on me, haven't you, Jillie?"

She saw Audrey curling up in the nearby chair, her frenzy over her agent's call forgotten.

"He's not a nice man, Mother."

Audrey chuckled. "Mmm. Even better. Lovey, if you're having trouble pinning him down, perhaps I could . . ."

Jillian tossed the cool cloth onto the coffee table and sat up on the couch, wincing against the bolt of pain throbbing in her temples from the sudden movement. She looked into wide green eyes that were already turning dreamy in anticipation of manipulating Jillian's life as if it were one more floundering scene. Audrey Tate, director.

"Mother, I don't need your help. I definitely don't need your help." The glazed-over look in Audrey's eyes made it clear that she wasn't getting through to Audrey. Once again. She snapped her fingers and waved her hand in front of her mother's face. "Listen up, Mother. It's time for a little stage direction."

Audrey turned to her with a breezy smile. "I'm sorry. You were saying?"

"I was saying that while you are here, you are not to interfere with my life. You do not grant interviews or call press conferences or do anything else to turn my life into a circus." Jillian could tell from her mother's benign smile that very little of this was registering. "Mother, don't you get it? I'm trying to lead a normal life here."

Audrey merely shook her head. "Oh, my. How incredibly dull. I truly have been a miserable failure as a mother, haven't I, lovey?"

Jillian sighed and sank back onto the couch. It was hopeless. Damage control was the best she could hope for. Keeping Audrey under wraps as much as possible. As soon as this headache went away, she would talk to Rosa. Maybe Rosa could help.

9

JILLIAN COULDN'T IMAGINE that her feet would ever again feel like anything except nubs of red-hot agony.

"Lose the five-inch heels," Rosa had warned as Jillian had headed out the front door for the one-hundred-dollar-a-plate celebrity-waiter dinner at the country club.

"No way. I go to great pains to hide the fact that I'm shorter than the average fifth-grader," Jillian had protested, giving her curls—today's color was a coppery red about the shade of a rusty penny—one last fluff and a spritz of lacquer. "You worry about keeping my mother under wraps and I'll worry about my aching feet."

Right now, as she balanced another silver tray full of haute cuisine she was too tired even to salivate over, she hoped Rosa was having better luck entertaining her mother than she was having with her feet. This bash to benefit multiple sclerosis was a great idea in theory, but Jillian had learned to appreciate just how tough it was to maintain her balance, her smile and her wit while delivering plates of poached salmon to Tallahassee's upper crust.

And it hadn't grown any easier when she'd realized that one of her fellow waiters was Russ Flynn.

You were surprised? she egged herself as she set the last crystal dish of crème caramel in front of the sequined chest of one of Florida's most controversial politicians. She headed back to the kitchen with her empty tray. *DJs do not shoot to the top of the ratings by good material alone.*

She dropped her tray onto a counter. That was it. Dessert was served. She was free for—she glanced at the Wonder Woman watch on her wrist—at least five minutes before she had to start gathering the dessert dishes.

Leaning against the counter, she bent over and slipped one instrument of torture off. A mistake, she knew, but she would worry about that later. Right now, a quick massage would be worth killing for.

"I can't believe you didn't bring your mother tonight. That would have been quite a coup—think of the publicity."

Jillian straightened at the sound of Russ's voice, almost toppling as she balanced on one foot. "Leave her out of this."

He glared at her, looking even more delectable than the crème caramel, in his white dinner jacket, which accentuated the olive darkness of his skin. Audrey was right. He was quite a morsel.

"I get it. You'll want to orchestrate this announcement very carefully." He put his tray down on top of hers. "For maximum impact. Why dilute the story by making it part of the charity coverage?"

She dropped her shoe to the floor and tried to slip her foot inside. Swollen, it refused to be crammed back into its leather casing. She wasn't sure which irritated her more—the foot or the know-it-all smugness on Russ Flynn's face.

"I said leave her out of this. I'm not looking for maximum impact and if— What are you doing?"

He looked up at her as if to say what he was doing must be fairly apparent. He had squatted beside her and taken her ankle in one hand and her shoe in the other. With gentle hands, he was massaging her toes and the sole of her foot before easing it slowly into the shoe.

"You must be crazy, wearing these shoes to a footrace like this." She didn't miss the faint grin as he turned to the other foot, slipping it out of its shoe and gently massaging it. "But you'd better not wait too long, you know."

"What?" Damned if she could follow a thing he was saying. She couldn't be sure if it was because he wasn't making much sense or because his hands on her foot felt so good. So exquisitely good. The goodness traveled up her ankle and all the way to her thigh. She shook off the sensations rushing into forbidden terrain. "What are you talking about?"

He slipped her other shoe back on and stood. It would take much more than five-inch heels to give her an advantage with Russ, she realized sourly.

"If you wait too long, maybe I'll steal your thunder. I know, it might sound like suicide to put the word out myself. But at least I'd be in the spotlight, too, when Tallahassee gets the news that you're practically royal blood—at least in the world of entertainment."

"Don't you dare!"

Now his grin was more than faint. It was spreading, blossoming into that ear-to-ear grin that was so maddening—and so appealing. She wanted to shove him right into the stack of dirty dishes behind him—then jump him; and kiss him senseless.

The knowledge that she still wanted him stoked the anger and desire that had flared from the instant she saw him.

Russ was still grinning. "Oh, a dare. I like a dare."

"I'm warning you, Russ Flynn. My private life is off-limits. You bring my private life into this and I'll...I'll..."

"You've already threatened to bury me," he goaded calmly. "What more can you do?"

"You don't want to find out."

Apparently he wasn't intimidated by her threats. He edged closer. They were almost chest to chest. She had to tilt her head at an uncomfortable angle to look him in the eye. When she did, his eyes were so close, it felt like they were staring into her soul while his warm breath escaped from lips that were equally close.

"I didn't know your private life was so precious."

"Now you know." The toughness had gone out of her voice. She knew that, but didn't know what to do about it. "So play fair."

"Play fair? You're a fine one to insist on fair play, J.T."

"You don't understand, Russ. It's . . . You don't understand." Damn him. He had melted all her toughness. She was jelly, pure and simple, aching to melt into his touch. Worse, she almost relished the prospect of losing control and surrendering what had been the most sacred part of her life for as long as she could remember. She wanted to spill every detail of her real life, even though she knew he was the last person in the world to expose them to. She wanted to open a heart that was beginning to hurt from so much hiding, from so much loneliness.

And—fool that she was—she kept telling herself that Russ Flynn was the one man she could trust with the whole truth. He would understand, she told herself, because he'd let her get a glimpse of the parts of his heart that he hid, too.

But giving in to her urge to open her heart, she knew, would be an even bigger mistake than what had already happened.

His hand, big and warm and comforting, closed around the side of her neck. Unconsciously she leaned into it. Her eyes closed. Comfort seeped in. And the fire in her flared higher. A new fire. Not the fire of anger; the fire only he could build in her. A fire that swept through her loins and burned away all her good sense, all her carefully wrought defenses.

"Then tell me," he whispered.

She didn't know who leaned forward, perhaps both of them. But his whisper ended against her mouth and she was powerless to pull away. His lips, warm and soft and urging, brushed over hers, brushed over her eyelids, brushed against her temple.

"If I don't understand, tell me, my Tallahassee Lassie."

Of course. That was why he wanted to understand—because she was the Tallahassee Lassie and he was the one she'd been brought here to crush. Jillian pulled back from the touch she craved—craved like a drug that would seduce her with its pleasures, then destroy her life.

Mustering the hardest look she could manage at the moment, she stared him down. She saw the tenderness in his blue eyes fade to disappointment; she almost gave in again.

Get tough, she told herself. "Stay out of my private life, Russ. That's all I have to say. Get out and stay out."

She grabbed her tray and left as quickly as her aching feet would allow. Her heart pounding, her stomach twisting with apprehension, she only hoped he believed her.

Lord knows, if he did, it had been her finest performance yet.

A PART OF RUSS SAID he had to take decisive action, do something bold and conclusive—a Clark Gable, matinee-idol kind of move that would leave Jillian's head spinning. Another part of him said he should simply forget her. That part of him was much less convincing.

But it was Howie who helped him make up his mind, the next afternoon at the Youth Center.

"I won't be here for a couple of days," Howie announced, his gaze avoiding Russ's. "Maybe more. I'm not sure."

"Why not?"

"I got stuff to do." The boy's dark eyes were lowered, denying Russ access to his feelings.

"What kind of stuff?"

Howie squirmed at Russ's insistence, his usual reluctance to make waves surfacing. Still, he held his ground. "Stuff. Important stuff."

Losing his patience with people who didn't trust him enough to tell him about their demons, Russ pushed Howie onto the bench and squatted in front of him, forcing eye contact. "That's not good enough, man. I want to know why you won't be around, and I want to know now."

Howie was silent a long time, but Russ could see his reticence breaking down. "I got to find my old lady."

"Your mother's gone again?"

"Yeah." Howie rubbed a hand over his head. "She said she'd be back last night, but she didn't make it. She said not to come looking for her when she takes off. And that's—I never do. I always do what she says. But I'm getting worried about her. You know?"

"Yeah. I know." Russ ached with the need to help. But how? "What can I do?"

Alarm flared in Howie's eyes. "Nothing. I got to do this myself. She looks funny. Kind of out of it. Like her eyes aren't paying attention. I worry sometimes. Maybe she's . . . I got to do this myself. I don't want to get her in trouble. Understand?"

Russ understood. Of all the kids in Youth Power, Howie was the one who always wanted to smooth over problems, who never wanted to stir things up. But right now, his reasons were even more compelling than merely seeking approval. Right now, Howie was afraid his mother was on drugs. And outside interference could send her out of his life a lot more permanently than her periodic disappearances. He patted his young friend on the knee. "Maybe you should do what she says. Stay out of it."

Russ saw from the look on Howie's face that the teen knew the dangers of trying to save his mother if drugs were her problem. Howie shook his head. "No, man. Sometimes you just got to jump in feet first, even if you've been told to stay out of it."

And as Russ parked his motorcycle in front of the condos later that afternoon, he knew Howie was right. It was time for Russ Flynn to play matinee idol.

He dashed to his condo, showered and pulled on fresh jeans. Then he rummaged through the fridge, grabbing two packs of cheese, two apples, grapes, and the bottle of wine he'd been saving for goodness knows what. Within thirty minutes, he was walking back out the door with a well-laden basket and two helmets and heading up the sidewalk to Jillian's condo.

Doubting his sanity and certain only that he was at least marginally safer than Howie would be in his quest, Russ pounded on the door. Instead of the cautious parting of the door that he'd grown accustomed to with Jillian, the door was abruptly flung open. He stared into Audrey's bright green eyes.

"Oh, too bad." Her pout was a half-flirty smile. "I don't suppose this is for me, is it?"

He grinned back. "Actually, this is a kidnapping."

"How exciting. Do come in." As Audrey closed the door behind him, Jillian walked in from the bedroom. "Look, lovey, he's come to kidnap you. Isn't that romantic?"

"I am not interested in being kidnapped."

"Of course not." Russ walked over to her, dropped his extra helmet over her softly braided hair, and pointed a finger at her through his jacket pocket. "That's why I'm armed."

"That is not a gun."

"Oh, lovey, I wouldn't argue with him if I were you. He looks dangerous to me."

Russ liked this woman—sometimes more than he liked her daughter. "She's right. I am dangerous."

"I know that. Now, why don't you—"

"Just come along quietly and no one will get hurt." He took her by the elbow and maneuvered her toward the door.

"You're the only one who's going to get hurt," Jillian hissed. But she followed him to the door anyway.

"Don't be silly. I'm much bigger than you are. Especially without those ridiculous shoes you were wearing last night."

She did, however, balk at the door.

"Just keep moving and nobody gets hurt," he urged.

"This is crazy," she said between clenched teeth.

"I know. Isn't it great?"

"Now, Jillie, just do what the man says and I'm sure everything will be fine."

She balked again when he led her to the motorcycle. "Why are you doing this?"

His own helmet still hanging from his arm, he reached down to buckle the strap of hers under her chin. On impulse, he dropped a kiss on her nose at the same time. He grinned as she frowned. "So you won't injure the pavement if you jump off the back and hit your hard little head."

"Not the helmet. This whole thing." She remained standing, feet planted firmly, while he straddled the bike.

"Get on."

"No."

"You're not going to make me tie you up and fling you over the back, are you? I always did like old cowboy movies."

"Why?"

"Why the hell do you think?"

She locked gazes with him. And when he was certain she couldn't mistake the longing in his eyes, she looked away, then swung one short leg over the bike and perched as far back on the seat as possible.

With one hand, he reached behind him, cupped her backside and slid her toward him. Her thighs were snug against his buttocks, her breasts soft against his back. He felt the tentative, barely-there motion of her hands resting at his waist.

And he was satisfied.

"Are you ready?"

The silence was a long one. When she spoke, he heard timidity fighting with her usual control. "Ride 'em, cowboy."

JILLIAN HAD NEVER understood the mystique of the motorcycle. But as they sped gracefully down the highway to the countryside south of Tallahassee, leaning into the curves, feeling one with the wind, she began to sense the excitement.

Or was it the excitement of having her arms around Russ? she wondered, loosening the hold that had grown progressively tighter.

The passing countryside seemed fingertip close without the normal barrier of a car windshield between it and her. Marshlands and farmlands were dotted with Spanish moss-draped live oaks. They sped through a small town, the quiet of its main street of gas station, general store and elementary school momentarily broken by the roar of the cycle's engine. Santiago, Pop. 1,439, the town-limits sign had read.

Just past the small cluster of houses and businesses were farms. At a narrow state road beside one of the farmhouses, Russ turned off the main highway. He slowed as he passed the house, a small white clapboard with a line of white sheets flapping in the spring breeze.

"Stately Flynn Manor," he called over his shoulder, gesturing toward the house.

Looking more closely at the low, neat stack of firewood and the bed of just-blooming flowers beside the building, Jillian felt a moment of panic. No. Surely to goodness he couldn't be taking her to meet his parents. Surely not that.

But he kept going. A few hundred yards past the house, he turned once again, this time down a narrow dirt road. Slowing to accommodate the ruts and bumps, Russ pushed on through thick vegetation. Through the trees, Jillian could see a small herd of grazing cows.

Russ stopped in front of a two-story plank house, unpainted and unoccupied, but showing no signs of neglect.

Jillian gazed at it while she unbuckled her helmet. She was tempted to wait until Russ offered some explanation. But he was silent while he turned off the bike's engine and hung their helmets over the handlebars. Then, retrieving the basket he'd strapped to the back of the bike, he pointed the way down a path leading away from the house.

Obviously, if she wanted any answers, it was her move. "Where are we?"

"My place."

"Ah. We must be here to look at your etchings."

"You must've missed the sign."

"What sign?"

"The one that said Posted: No Wisecracking." He dropped the basket to the ground a few hundred feet from a pond. Then he pulled a worn blanket from the basket and spread it out.

"No wisecracking. That'll leave you seriously hampered, won't it?"

"Maybe." He was hiding a grin as he sat down and started pulling things out of the basket. "Although, actually, I think I'm better equipped for real conversation than you are."

"You? The master of the glib quip?"

He shook his head. "I thought I was the master. But a few weeks ago, I met someone who's even better than me at hiding behind clever repartee. Now, sit."

"Is that an order?"

He looked up, his eyes softening. "Won't you join me, Jillie?"

She lowered herself to the blanket and helped him unwrap fruit and cheese. Then he uncorked the bottle of wine and poured it into two paper cups.

"So, tell me about your place."

"Actually, it was my great-grandfather's place. He built it around the turn of the century. With his own hands." He pointed across the pond, where the tangle of Spanish moss and twisted cypress branches grew thicker, wilder. "The place backs onto Wakulla Springs, a freshwater spring. I was the world's most intrepid explorer about twenty-five years ago, before I discovered radio. Granddad had a million stories about the times they filmed Tarzan movies there, back in the thirties."

She waited.

"Nobody's lived in it since my grandmother died in 1975. It got kind of rough around the edges for a few years, with nobody to see after it."

"But now you're taking care of it."

He nodded.

"And someday . . . ?"

He looked at her and smiled, as if pleased that she understood there was more. "And someday I'm going to get the plumbing straightened out and rig up a woodburning stove in the fireplace for heat."

"And live here."

He hesitated. "And raise a family here. It's a great place for raising a family. Away from . . . everything."

She had to agree with that. Just imagining such an idyllic childhood made her envious.

"And WKIX?"

He grinned ruefully. "I thought you were going to solve that conflict for me."

"No wisecracking," she reminded him.

"Okay, no wisecracking." He studied the bottom of his paper-cup wineglass for answers. "I'm getting tired of it. I'm getting tired of being at the mercy of people's whims about what's hot and what's not. I'm tired of eating my gut out every thirteen weeks, worrying if a bunch of nameless people are tired of listening to me."

"What will you do?"

His laugh was soft. "Aye, there's the rub. What do I want to be when I grow up?" Sliding closer on the blanket, he popped a plump red grape between her lips. "And what do you want to be when you grow up, Jillie?"

"That's easy. Just what I am."

"Not a big star?" He sounded skeptical.

"Follow in Mother's footsteps, you mean?" She leaned on one elbow and stared intently over the pond. "No way."

"Worried you won't measure up?"

"No. More worried that I might."

"What's that mean?"

She rolled onto her stomach and plucked a dandelion growing at the edge of the blanket. "Let's just say I'm not cut out to be the big star—and leave it at that."

"No, let's not. I want to hear it, Jillian. It's part of the riddle, and I'm ready for the answer."

She didn't even have to ask what he meant. She'd been trying to fool herself for too long that she was holding out on Russ because of who he was, where he worked. But it was getting harder and harder to fool herself. Keeping secrets had become an obsession with her—an obsession that had ruled her life for far too long; an obsession that Russ Flynn made her want to overcome.

It was time to open up. Trust. So she plunged in.

"All right. It means I'd wade out into that pond right now and drown myself if I thought I had to spend the rest of my life in the kind of spotlight she's in."

"Aren't you in the spotlight?"

"Not the kind she's in. Believe me, it's not the same."

"How do you know?"

"Because I grew up inside the circle of her spotlight. I know. I know."

With a gentle motion, he swept her into his arms. His lips lowered to hers, capturing hers in a kiss that was nothing like the others they had shared. It was gentle, demanding in a way that had nothing to do with passion. It was a kiss that demanded trust, and promised to reciprocate.

"Tell me about it, my Tallahassee Lassie."

Telling him about it, she knew, might be the biggest mistake she could make. But so could not telling him about it.

10

Russ felt himself, foolishly, holding his breath. These few moments, while Jillian sat there on his faded FSU stadium blanket, obviously at war with herself, seemed somehow foreboding.

Would she accept his friendship, and demonstrate it by revealing the secrets she sheltered so zealously? Or would she do what she'd always done before—shut him out with a flippant retort or the defensive anger that flared so easily when she felt cornered?

And why the hell should it matter?

Russ wasn't sure he liked the answer that occurred to him.

"What was your childhood like, Russ?"

Not the response he'd been expecting. He frowned, but as he took in her solemn expression, he knew his answer was somehow part of her answer.

"Typical." Even as he spoke the word, the connection dawned on him. "Dad farmed a little and managed the local feed store. Mom was the perfect farm wife—which meant she could do everything from run the tractor to can enough corn and green beans to see us through the winter, and keep a couple of not-so-perfect kids from running wild in the streets."

Jillian nodded, but didn't return his smile.

"I wasn't a bad kid, but I wasn't exactly model-son material, either. Hated school. And managed to cut more classes then I went to, some years. My grades weren't bad, but that was mostly because I knew how to play the game and feed my teachers whatever B.S. they were looking for." He laughed softly, pleased at last to see a wistful smile curving her lips. "Mom chose to believe it was because I was smarter than my grades proved. Anyway, I managed to graduate without breaking any major laws. And spent one quarter at FSU, mostly to satisfy Mom. But I wasn't college material."

"Wasn't? Or didn't want to risk trying to be?"

"Say, I thought this was your turn on the couch, not mine." There she went again, cutting right to the heart. Life with Jillian would never be safe and complacent, he decided. *Where the hell had a thought like that come from, anyway?* "What does this have to do with you?"

"Not a darn thing." A hint of wry bitterness tinged her words. "That's just the point. Not a darn thing."

Now it was his time to wait—while she made up her mind.

She drew a deep breath. She had decided to bare a little of her soul, he realized jubilantly, but it wasn't going to be easy.

"I don't suppose you spent much time on the national news, trying to look grown-up and unconcerned while your mother dismissed her marriage to your father as 'just one of those ghastly follies we all commit in our youth,'" she said blandly. The only outer indication of her emotions was the corner of the blanket she twisted in one fist. "I don't suppose you had to listen very often while your classmates made up jump-rope rhymes about your mother's many marriages."

She laughed tonelessly. "There was a young woman who lived in a shoe, she had so many husbands she didn't know what to do."

Russ flinched. In his mind, he could see Jillian as a child, learning to control every reaction while her schoolmates played at taunting her.

"One kid—she was my best friend that year—brought in a scrapbook she'd been keeping of all the tabloid stories about my mother. She was so proud of it. I don't think she ever understood why we weren't so close after that." Jillian paused. "It was too bad, really—she was one of the few girls whose mother didn't object to her playing with me. Most of them didn't want their little darlings hanging around me. No telling what kind of Hollywood depravity I'd picked up at home, you know."

"You're kidding? People don't really think that way, do they?" But he knew, as he saw the little-girl-lost look in her eyes, that some people thought exactly that way.

"You know, I was invited to exactly one birthday party my whole childhood." A wry smile tugged at her lips. "Mother showed up while the ice cream and cake were being served. Which was okay, except that she had a TV camera crew in tow. They were shooting one of those 'at home with' kind of shows and she wanted America to see what a typical, loving mother she was. Disrupted the whole party."

She sighed and smiled—a smile that was at the same time both accepting and incredulous. "So I learned pretty early that it was easier all around if I . . . didn't even try to pretend I was normal."

She stopped and, looking down at her hands, seemed to realize what she'd been doing to the blanket. She dropped the wrinkled flannel, but didn't look up. "I thought things were changing when I started high school. The boys— Suddenly it seemed everybody wanted to date me. It didn't take long to realize why—they all assumed I'd act as wild as the tabloids said my mother acted."

Stretching out beside her, Russ put a hand on her shoulder. "Didn't your mother—I mean, wasn't there something she could have done?"

Tears glistened in her thickly lashed eyes. She blinked them away. "I guess not. I don't know. I'm not sure she was there enough to understand. She was always off filming a movie. She always whirled into town with expensive gifts and lots of big talk about the trips we were going to take together. Then another movie would come along and she was gone. I used to blame her." She smiled faintly. "Let's be honest here. I still do, sometimes. But not nearly as much as I did when I was ten."

Russ pulled her to him, felt her heart pounding against his chest.

"But you love her anyway?"

"Of course, I do. She's funny and childish and adorable. As long as you aren't expecting her to be a good mother, she's irresistible."

He held her close for a long time, in silence, hearing the pain that was so intimately wrapped up in the flippant way she spoke of her mother.

"And that's why I didn't want you to know who I was." She leaned her head into the crook of his shoulder. "That's why I left Atlanta—because one of the reporters up there was closing in on the story. And once people know who I am, it's just like being little Jillie Joyner again. My life is part of somebody's show-and-tell. Part of recess on the playground."

He knew that her fingers roamed his chest unconsciously, and he closed his eyes to shut out his automatic reaction. "Then why radio? This doesn't make sense. Why not teach school or be a librarian or an accountant? If you hate publicity so much, why put yourself out there where it's bound to come?"

"Because I love it. I love performing. It's in my blood, I guess. But my skin's just not thick enough to take the public dissection that comes with it."

The words came unbidden. "Your skin's not thick at all." He knew it was so. Her skin was satin soft. Everywhere. Including the cheek pressed to his neck. And other places he was better off not thinking about right now.

She laughed quietly and he was astonished at his gladness. Oh, Lord, he was in such trouble. His heart soared at the signal her mood had lightened. But he didn't want that. He didn't want his heart involved in this at all.

Too late, his heart whispered to him. *Too late for that*.

Her hand, which had strayed over his chest, igniting desire, now moved upward. A finger stroked his lower lip. He felt himself stir. He warned himself to back away.

But it was too late for that, too.

Her voice was a whisper of breath against his neck. "Thank you. Thank you for listening and understanding."

He searched for a flippant answer. None came to him. The connection between brain and tongue, it seemed, had shut down. His next words were proof of that. "I think I love you, Jillie."

She tensed in his arms. But the leaping response of his body paid no mind to her instant of rebuttal.

"Don't say that."

"I think I love you, Jillie." And his stubborn insistence freed something inside him. He laughed now, pulling away to look into her heart-shaped face and the confusion in her eyes—a confusion that matched what he'd felt just moments before. He laughed again and raised a hand to caress her cheek. "I think I love you, Jillie, and you can't stop me."

She laughed back, the confusion in her eyes easing only slightly. "You're crazy. Do you know that? You're crazy."

A big drop of rain splashed on her cheek beside his thumb. Then another.

He kissed a drop on the tip of her nose. "Uh-oh. It's the daily deluge."

More raindrops. Big ones. Coming faster. She moved to get up, but he grasped her more tightly to him.

"Stay here. I like making love when you're wet."

Now her laughter was more confident. She pushed against his chest and this time he let her go.

"You *are* crazy," she said as she leaped up and started shoving things into the basket.

Within minutes, they were running through a downpour, back down the path toward the farmhouse. But instead of heading for Russ's motorcycle, he led her up the plank steps and into the house. Dropping their basket and blankets, they stood dripping on the bare wooden floor, laughing and unable to take their eyes off each other.

When he took a step in her direction, her laughter grew breathless and she backed away.

"Oh, no, you don't," she said, retreating another step as he tried again to close the space between them. Her eyes were alight with mischief. "I know what you're up to. You've lured me out here to this isolated spot. And now you plan to take advantage of me. Well, I'm not that easy, buster. You can just—"

He lunged at her, but she jumped beyond his reach. "You're mine, now," he murmured ominously. "I've got you right where I want you."

She purred seductively at his mock threat, but leaped away once again as he moved toward her. "You'll never catch me."

Then she ran. In a circle through the downstairs rooms he chased her, growling threats as she squealed and giggled. She dashed up the stairs and he followed, halting momentarily as something covered his face. He pulled it away and stared down at the knit shirt she'd been wearing. He grinned. Three steps higher, he stumbled over a scrap of ivory-colored lace. He paused again, grinning as he held it to his face and breathed in her fragrance. He hardened instantly as the perfume that was distinctly Jillian filled his nostrils.

Moving slowly now, he topped the stairs. She had disappeared into one of the bedrooms, but he followed the trail. Two canvas shoes. A pile of denim. And, right outside the last room on the left, another scrap of ivory lace. His heart was pounding painfully fast as he entered the room.

It was empty except for an iron bed covered by an old feather mattress. But before he could back out of the room, he was tackled from behind. With a gleeful shout, she jumped out of hiding, throwing herself at him and locking her arms and legs around him. He staggered forward and they fell into the soft thickness of the feather bed, laughing as they tugged at his clothes.

"Who's got who?" she teased, rubbing her breasts against his chest as she pushed his shirt aside.

"Who's crazy now?" he countered, groaning as she moved over him. He cupped her thatch of red-brown curls, easing a finger deep inside her moist warmth. She gasped, and the hands that tugged at his zipper momentarily stilled. "Don't get lazy now, woman."

Half laugh, half sigh signaled her awareness of his discomfort. Working frenetically, she rid him of his jeans and straddled him again.

"I'll teach you to threaten me with love, you libertine," she taunted, stroking his nipples with her fingers while she continued to undulate back and forth.

"Oh, yes," he urged, reaching up to cover a gently swaying breast. "Teach me."

She shook her head and removed his hand. "Naughty boy," she whispered, pinning both hands over his shoulders. The movement brought her heavy breasts close to his face. Close, but not close enough. He reached for a dark, taut peak with his tongue, but couldn't make contact. "Look, but don't touch," she warned, her eyes still filled with mischief.

So he played her game, letting her pin him to the bed with her feather-light touch, and found that the forbidden closeness of her satiny skin drove his passion almost to the breaking point. She taunted him, skimming herself softly over his penis, sliding her breasts against the sides of his face. A wild groan burst from him. Still holding his hands, she lowered her head and captured one of his nipples between her teeth. Calling her name, he arched against her, aching to bury himself in her. But still she played coy, continuing to tease at his nipple, then trailing a few soft kisses lower over his chest.

"Now, if you're very good," she murmured, "I'll let you go. But you have to promise."

"I promise," he vowed, his voice hoarse.

She laughed. "You don't even know what you're promising."

"Anything. Anything."

She laughed again and he felt her hands release his wrists and caress his arms, then move to his chest, as her mouth crept even lower. "Promise to be very still. And let me have my way with you."

He smiled even as he groaned at the moist trail she was leaving down the middle of his belly.

"Very still," he vowed softly, then broke his promise with an involuntary shudder as her lips brushed against the swollen tip of his penis.

"Naughty, naughty." He felt her warm breath against him as she reminded, "You promised to be still."

But he couldn't get another word out as she flicked her tongue over him. Incoherent groans were all he was capable of for the next few minutes. And by the time she raised herself over him once again and eased their bodies together, Russ knew he had never, ever come close to the magic this woman was working on his body.

He was only faintly aware of her cry of pleasure as she buried him inside her moist warmth. He knew only that he throbbed against her, close to completion. Grasping her hips to still her in hopes of prolonging their union, he whispered, "This won't be long enough, I'm afraid."

But as he gazed into her eyes, Russ knew he was both right and wrong. This wouldn't last nearly long enough. And, if he had his way, it would last forever.

He delayed his climax only long enough to be sure she was with him, giving in to a wild-eyed release that he felt certain went far deeper than the flesh. Incoherent cries that bordered on anguish burst from her lips as her body convulsed, grasping him tightly and frantically. He gloried in her climax as much as his own, and when she collapsed against his chest, damp and gasping for breath, he wrapped his arms around her shoulders and absorbed the rhythm of her pounding heart.

When she stirred away from him, Russ prayed it didn't signal her emotional withdrawal. But she snuggled against his side, and he was grateful for their continued intimacy.

"Thank you," he whispered.

"Thank you? Oh, I was expecting a much more formal acknowledgement. An engraved note, perhaps, and a dozen red—"

"Thank you for trusting me that much."

He saw the embarrassment in her face. "Oh. Well . . ."

"For trusting me enough to let go, to let me see your emotions."

She flushed and her voice was barely audible when she spoke. "Thank you, Russ, for being someone I can trust."

He tightened his hold on her. The only thing he could think of to say now was the one thing he felt instinctively would turn her off. "Do you think I'm someone you can . . . love?"

All he could see was the top of her head, her curls in tumbled disarray. When she didn't answer right away, he continued. "Because I think— That is— I probably need to know, before I . . . do something foolish."

"Like what?"

"Like fall in love with you."

She edged a few inches away from him, so their bodies weren't pressed so intimately together. Her eyes, filled with fear and longing and hope, gazed into his. "Maybe you shouldn't do that, Russ."

He wondered if it wasn't too late to do anything about it. Unwilling to accept the physical distance she was trying to create, he left one hand on her back and used the other to trace the round, smooth curve of her cheek. "So I'm not someone you think you could love?"

She closed her eyes and leaned into his touch, with a look of fresh desire on her face. "I didn't say that."

His fingers strayed from her cheek to her neck, then wandered along the curve of her bare shoulder. Warmth spread through him and he saw her body surrendering to his touch. "Come here, Jillian. Let me love you."

She took his hand and held it back to her face, dropping a damp kiss into its center. "You won't rush me, will you?"

"Not this time. This time, we'll take it slow."

AS THE MOTORCYCLE ROARED through the night air, Jillian contentedly wrapped her arms around Russ's waist, pressed her thighs tightly to his hips.

But as soon as she unlocked the front door of her condo and they walked in, the contentment vanished, to be replaced by anxiety. Audrey, wrapped in a slinky silk kimono, was stretched out on the couch, the telephone attached to her ear.

Jillian was too familiar with the impatient and slightly bored voice her mother was using. She'd heard it too many times—usually right before Audrey announced that it was time to see an attorney; usually right before the reporters camped out on the front lawn.

"How can you say that?" Audrey smiled at them, gesturing impatiently at the voice on the other end of the telephone line. "Of course, my career is important, Henry. But how can you say it's more important to me than—"

Audrey stopped abruptly. Jillian looked away. Russ slipped an arm lightly around her shoulder. But she didn't want the comfort his touch offered, not here. Here, she didn't want to need the comfort. Here, she wanted to be immune to any need for comfort.

Then why aren't you immune? "I guess you'd better go."

He pulled her against him. "I thought maybe you'd stay with me tonight."

The length of his body, touching hers lightly, revived tempting memories.

The sound of Audrey, slamming the phone down with disgust, startled Jillian. "I don't think so."

She inched away from Russ, and stood with her arms crossed over her chest.

"That man is so spineless." Audrey swept past them on her way to the kitchen. "Imagine! He blames me for all this. He knew who I was when he married me, for goodness' sake!"

It isn't over, Jillian thought. *It's never over.*

Jillian looked at Russ—at the face she'd first come to know through billboards and other publicity. She reminded herself how public her own life had been since she'd rubbed shoulders with him. And how much more public it could get, if she wasn't careful. *At least you don't have to perpetuate it in your own life, with a man who belongs to the public.*

"This afternoon was lovely, Russ." She couldn't deny it, didn't even want to deny it. "But don't start expecting anything more."

She couldn't tell if the flash in his blue eyes indicated hurt or anger. It came and went, leaving behind a look filled with an understanding she felt too vulnerable to accept. He reached out and traced her jaw with his fingers.

"It's too late for that. Don't you know that, Jillie?"

11

WITH HER MOTHER IN the house, Jillian couldn't bring herself to stay with Russ overnight. But her desire to be with him was stronger than her nagging apprehension about their relationship.

Over the next week, they spent long hours together. Jillian discovered they were both happy with quiet walks in the country and afternoons at home with videos or old black-and-white movies. Russ even treated Audrey like a down-to-earth mother instead of a star—a novel response that made it easier for Jillian to feel comfortable with him around.

Each day that passed drew Jillian closer to a realization she would have preferred not making. Her days were incomplete without Russ. Her life was incomplete without Russ.

But her concerns about needing to keep her distance from him didn't subside. Even snuggled beside him in his bed, shades drawn to dim the afternoon sunshine, she couldn't suppress them.

"What is it, Jillian? What's wrong?"

"Nothing's wrong."

But she didn't protest when he turned her on her belly, straddled her and started gently massaging her back and shoulders.

"Something's wrong. We've just spent the afternoon making love and you're so wound up, the muscles in your neck are like a clenched fist. Tell me what's wrong."

She sighed. He was right, of course. Their lovemaking was only a temporary reprieve from all the worries plaguing her.

His hands stilled and she murmured a protest.

"That's all you get until you tell me what's on your mind."

Eyes closed, still conscious of his body poised above hers, Jillian drew a deep breath. "You know what tomorrow is?"

She could tell from the silence that followed her question—he knew exactly what tomorrow was. And it was as much on his mind as it was on hers.

She answered for him. "The ratings come out tomorrow."

"The ratings have nothing to do with us, Jillie."

She would have laughed except for the hollow tone of his claim. "The ratings have everything to do with us and you know it."

He lay down beside her, pulling her close to him. "The ratings have to do with Jammin' J.T. and Russ for Rush Hour—nothing to do with Jillian and Russ. Got it?"

"No, Russ. We both know better than that. The ratings have everything to do with us. The ratings can destroy us. The ratings rule us. You know that."

"My love for you isn't ruled by the ratings, Jillie."

"Don't say that." She squirmed in his arms, but he held her fast.

"Don't say what? I love you? I do. I love you. And the ratings can't change that."

"The ratings can change everything. You know that."

"Can the ratings make you love me?"

"Russ, don't—"

"Okay, okay. I'm a patient man." He kissed her—a slow, soft kiss that almost made her forget the ratings. "And stop worrying about the ratings. If I'm not worried, why should you be? You're bound to make a good showing."

"And what does that do to you?"

"Don't worry about me. Listen, if it makes you feel any better, I'm looking at some other possibilities. We may not have to worry about being competitors much longer."

Then he kissed her again—a lingering, wet kiss that definitely made her forget the ratings.

WHEN JIM TOWERS WALKED into the control room during the middle of her shift, Jillian knew the day was off to a bad start.

Of course, she'd had that ominous feeling all morning, even as she'd showered and dressed. And now, the moment she'd been dreading had arrived. Towers had the ratings in his hand.

"So, looks like Mother Nature has bikinis in mind today for all you sun worshipers," Jillian said into the mike as she finished an update on the weather.

Towers perched on a stool across the control panel from her, coolly slipping through the papers, giving nothing away. An S.O.B. to the end, she thought.

"So the question remaining is this: Is bikini weather ready for you?" She plugged in the cart with the diet-center commercial spot, then closed her mike. While the ad ran, Towers sat before her in silence, never looking up. Loathe to give him what he wanted, still, she had to ask.

"Well? Should I pack up my gear? Or do you want me to hang around another thirteen weeks?"

He allowed satisfaction to soften his face. "We're up there. Number two behind Flynn, all the way up from number five."

Jillian wasn't even surprised at the sinking feeling in the pit of her stomach. She was supposed to be elated. But she hadn't really expected to be. Not anymore.

"And the margin between you and Flynn isn't much of a margin." Towers stood. "Another thirteen weeks and he'll be history at 'KIX."

Lips tightly drawn, Jillian prepared a song to fill the airspace following the diet-center commercial.

"You've done a damn good job. I like your strategy, but I don't think you've taken it far enough." His stony expression returned. "To make sure you pull in those last few points you need to take us over the top, I want you to step up the plan."

"What plan? What are you talking about?"

"The romance angle. There was another item in this morning's paper. I like it. Keep it up, see if you can't milk it for more publicity." He walked toward the door, then paused with his hand on the knob. "And when we've nailed the coffin shut on Flynn at 'KIX, I've got big plans for the two of you."

Her heartbeat became a panicky flutter. "What?"

"You'll make a great morning team. Unbeatable."

"You can't be serious! Russ would never go for that." *Would he?*

"Wouldn't he?" He smiled. "Do you really think he'd rather go under than team up?"

Towers walked out the door. The song ended. Jillian's mind was awhirl as she segued into the news at the top of the hour. What would Russ say to teaming up, if the alternative was being tossed off the air completely? What would anybody say?

And Towers had sounded so confident. Almost as if... Almost as if he already knew what Russ would say. Almost as if . . .

What was it Russ had said yesterday afternoon? *I'm looking at some other possibilities. We may not have to worry about being competitors much longer.*

Suddenly, all the ominous feelings with which she'd started the day seemed justified.

ANGER AND FEAR WARRED in Jillian as she drove into the parking lot at WKIX. Oblivious to the stares drawn by her knee-skimming jungle-print wrap dress as she stalked past the receptionist, Jillian prowled the halls of the country-music station until she found what she was looking for.

Russ was just walking into a production room, but he stopped, a pleased smile on his face, as Jillian rounded the corner. Putting her hand on his chest, she pushed him into the room ahead of her.

"What the—"

"What are you up to, Russ Flynn?" she demanded.

"What are you talking about?" He put his hands on her shoulders.

"And more to the point, how long have you been up to it? Could it be you've been so suspicious about my motives because yours haven't exactly been lily pure?"

He frowned and glanced over her head. Following his gaze, she discovered that a couple of people passing in the corridor had stopped to peer in the doorway. They grinned at Russ's discomfiture. With a stern expression on her face, Jillian marched back to the entrance.

"Excuse us, please," she said sweetly. "We're about to have major warfare and it won't be a pretty sight."

She closed the door. Then, just for good measure, she shoved the lock into place—a move she knew would light up the Taping In Progress signal outside. Their privacy was guaranteed.

"Now," she said, folding her arms over her chest and turning back to face Russ, "where was I? Oh, yes. Just when did you hatch this little plot of yours?"

"It would be a lot simpler if you'd tell me what little plot you're referring to." Apparently unconcerned, he leaned against the control panel, almost grinning. That didn't sit at all well with Jillian.

"Oh? Are there more than one? Do we need a score-card here?"

She moved closer to him, wishing she could find a way to wipe the deepening grin off his face. Damn his duplicity. Damn his eyes. They cut right to her soul, where the real emotion responsible for this show of anger resided. Betrayal—that's what she felt, deep down.

He reached out to finger the gold conch shell dangling from her left ear. "I always need a scorecard to keep up with you, Jillie."

"Don't call me Jillie." She shook off his touch, wondering how to get him to take her seriously. It couldn't be easy, she supposed, as long as his touch whispering close to her neck drew shivers. "Tell me the truth, Russ. This is all part of some big plan, isn't it?"

Now he reached with the other hand to cup the gold sand-dollar that hung from her other ear, and his knuckles brushed against her. Involuntarily, her eyes drifted shut in response to the wave of desire that washed through her. Too late, her eyes flew open; his look told her he knew that she was aroused. His fingers tangled in the tendrils of flame-colored curls feathering down her neck and over her ears.

"What's part of some big plan?"

She had to concentrate hard to take in the meaning of his question. "What is?" She repeated his words to give her time to think. She had to think, to find the right response. "This—" the word stuck in her throat "—seduction."

With his fingers around the back of her neck, he pulled her closer to him. He bent his face nearer to hers. "You mean *this* seduction?"

And his mouth lowered to hers. Hot and wet and demanding, his tongue parted her lips and invaded. She tried to find her anger, tried to feel the betrayal, but there was no fight in her. With his tongue mating with hers, with his arm behind her back drawing her closer inch by inch, she felt only the compulsion to meld with him.

Before he pulled her completely against him, Russ loosened the wide leather belt at her waist. It fell open and with it, the wrap dress fell away from her. His hands roamed beneath the fabric, bringing heightened sensations to the flesh beneath her satin-and-lace bodysuit. He ran his fingers along the lower edges of the suit, which was cut high on her thighs. He grazed the swell of her breasts over the sheer cups. Then he eased a hand between her legs, releasing the snaps.

"We can't," she gasped, nevertheless easing into his touch as he reached for her telltale moistness. "Not here."

"Oh, yes, we can."

She heard his zipper grind, then felt him, hot and hard, slipping into place between her legs. She groaned. He cradled her buttocks in his hands and sank into her.

"You are so evil," she whispered, wrapping her legs around his waist to take in every inch of him.

He grinned and slowly lowered them to the carpet and settled Jillian on her back before he started to move with her. She was hungry to see more flesh, feel more flesh, but something in the sight of him—sleeves rolled up to his elbows, necktie only slightly loose, leather belt properly in place—gave their lovemaking the deliciousness of the forbidden.

When she felt him quicken and swell inside her, felt him tense as the waves of release began, she would have cried out but for his hand that clamped over her mouth.

Still entangled, they rolled to one side. Then he uncovered her mouth. "Mind if we leave the sound effects out of this?"

She laughed softly. "You are evil. Do you know that?"

"Hey, if you come in here accusing me of seduction, don't expect me to play innocent." His lips caressed her breasts above the lace.

She hadn't wanted to be reminded—not while he was still buried in her and the scent of their lovemaking still hung in the air.

He lifted her chin so their gazes met. "Now that you're a little more rational, what the hell was this all about?"

What if she gave the wrong answer? Or what if the truth she saw in his eyes admitted to the betrayal? "Have you talked to Towers?"

"Who?"

So far, so good. He looked genuinely confused. She took a deep breath. "Jim Towers. My station manager."

"Should I have?"

Not a direct answer. Not so good. "Did he offer you a job?"

Now she was sure. He did look guilty. Or at least uncomfortable. "Why don't you just come out and tell me what you're accusing me of?"

"He wants you to be my partner. Is that why... why you... why we...?"

Russ frowned. "Did I lure you into bed because your boss wants to team us up on the air?"

When he said it that way, she felt rotten even having thought it. But she was in too far now. She had to know. Without a doubt. "Well, did you?"

"No."

The edge of anger in his voice reminded Jillian that she was lying on the floor in a production room of a rival radio station, her dress open down the front, her body damp with their lovemaking. That would top even the juiciest scandal Audrey had managed to embroil herself in over the years. As discreetly as possible, she adjusted her bodysuit and stood to rewrap her dress. She tried not to notice as he straightened his own clothes.

"No, Jillian. This isn't part of some grand scheme."

"But you have talked to Towers?"

"Towers talked to me." He ran a hand through his hair. "Months ago. Before you even showed up. Asked me to think about coming over to 'FLA. Asked if I'd be interested in teaming up, if they found the right person."

"And you said...?"

"Listen, I wasn't about to burn any bridges."

"So you said yes."

"I said maybe."

Jillian suddenly felt queasy. "Well, isn't this cozy!"

She turned to leave, but Russ grabbed her by the shoulders again. "Jillian, I swear, that never crossed my mind when we met."

She wanted to believe him. More than she'd ever wanted anything—more, even, than she'd wanted to live outside her mother's shadow—she wanted to believe him.

She nodded. "You heard about the ratings?"

"I might've known you'd rub that in."

His grin reassured her—a little, at least.

"How's the station reacting?"

His grin dimmed only slightly.

"They've been happier."

Unhappy enough to drop you? she wondered. And if WKIX bought out his contract, then what? What would he do if Towers's little arrangement was the only way he could stay in radio?

As she contemplated that possibility, Jillian admitted she wasn't sure she could walk away from Russ; even if it meant acting out their love life in public, she wasn't sure she could walk away from him.

And that was all it took to convince her she'd better get out while she had the willpower to do so.

JILLIAN'S ARMS WERE the only safe haven Russ could find during the next few days. At the station, everyone was acting strange. People either kept their distance because they didn't know what to say or were overly jocular just to prove nothing had changed. When a star begins to fall, Russ realized, nobody wants to go down with it.

He speculated, when he was alone and unable to escape his thoughts, whether he could face leaving Tallahassee in search of another radio job.

He speculated, as he talked by telephone with an employment counselor, whether he was qualified to do anything else with his life.

He speculated, when he held Jillian close, what she would do if Towers made a serious offer—and he considered it.

About the only thing he was sure of was whether he could live without Jillian: he couldn't.

So when he wasn't on the air, he wanted to be in her arms. And when he couldn't be in her arms, he did the next best thing. He tried to get close to Audrey. Perhaps, he told himself, the mother held more clues to the daughter than he'd imagined.

One afternoon, when they went out to the pool together, he was startled by Audrey's probing question.

"Do you think my daughter has an unusual preoccupation with avoiding publicity?" Audrey asked as she covered her redhead's complexion with the same heavy-duty sunscreen her daughter used.

Russ ducked underwater long enough to contemplate his answer. He wasn't sure his role here extended to mending fences between mother and daughter. On the other hand, if Jillian could resolve her relationship with her mother . . .

He sprang up out of the water and shook his head to clear his eyes. "Could be. Why?"

Audrey raised herself up from the lounge chair. "I know this sounds strange, but I get the strongest sense that she's trying to keep me under wraps while I'm here with her. Do you know, when I asked my agent to fly down so we could discuss this movie deal, I think she was ready to— Actually, what she said was, she would have me kidnapped and returned to Connecticut first."

She smiled—the impish little smile that America loved. "Now, isn't that silly?"

Russ smiled back at Audrey, who he was beginning to realize was surprisingly naive in many ways. He groped for a gentle way to say what needed to be said. A gentle way, because Jillian was right: It was impossible not to fall for Audrey.

"Maybe she feels like the publicity's made it hard for her to . . . live a normal life."

Audrey stared at him. "Are you in love with my daughter?"

When he hesitated, she narrowed her eyes and shook a long, silk-wrapped nail at him. "You are. And you needn't try to hide it."

Russ smiled. He tried for one incongruous moment to imagine Audrey Tate sitting down to fried chicken and mashed potatoes at his mother's dinette table. "Okay. I'm in love with her."

"Well, do you plan to marry her? You know, I don't believe in all this sleeping-around business. If you two are going to . . . be intimate . . . I believe you should marry her. You know, this is not common in the circles I frequent, but I've never— Well, I just believe in marriage."

Which made it easier to understand her five husbands. But the stern look in her eyes made it clear that she expected a response. Yet he wasn't ready to respond, simply because he knew it wasn't something Jillian was even remotely ready to consider.

He decided to dodge the question. "Are you offering her hand?"

Audrey grunted. "Now, that would be the kiss of death, Russell. If I suggest that she marry you, you'll never make it to the altar with my daughter."

She settled back and closed her eyes against the sun. But before Russ could slip back into the water, she suddenly waved her hand dismissively. "A normal life. Who in their right mind would want a normal life, anyway? Do you know how boring normal life can be?"

WHILE JILLIAN GLAD-HANDED at a furniture-store grand opening and worried what mischief her mother would get into, left on her own, Russ went to the Youth Center and took Audrey with him.

He had expected her to enjoy the motorcycle ride more than the center, even though she'd asked more than once about his work there. But when they entered the gym, he discovered that Audrey's interest in the project hadn't been feigned.

While he shot baskets with a small group of the regulars, she charmed a newcomer into a game of pool. Almost instantly her polished coyness disappeared and Audrey became one of the guys.

"That your old lady?" Howie stared wistfully after Audrey and the timid Cuban youth who followed in her wake.

"Audrey? No, she's just a friend." The wistful expression on Howie's face was an apt reminder that his own worries were minor compared to the ones Howie shouldered. "Any news on your mom?"

Howie's smile was brave but unconvincing. "Not yet. She'll be back soon. I— My aunt convinced me to stay out of it. I don't know if that's the right thing or not. But she said . . . she said I could just cause trouble for Mom. Reckon that's true?"

"Your aunt's smart, Howie."

Another young voice interrupted them. "Say, Russ, a dude with a bunch of cameras is looking for you."

Russ frowned. He didn't recognize the TV news reporter or the station call letters on the camera. Besides, he was in no mood to be "on" for publicity.

But the reporter's introduction surprised Russ. From a station in Jacksonville, he was working on a national roundup of efforts to keep today's youth in school.

"And I hear you've got a helluva program going right here," the reporter said, his eyes scanning the gym. "We'd like to cover what you're doing, if you can spare a few minutes to tell us about it."

Knowing the school board was interested in as much good publicity as possible for the program, Russ led the reporter and his cameraman through the gym. He explained what was happening with the students, and those who were interested were interviewed.

Only one person in the gym seemed determinedly uninterested in the reporter and his camera: Audrey. Whenever the camera was pointed in her direction, she made a point of turning her back and moving to another part of the center.

Perhaps Audrey's life in the public eye had in fact been as difficult for her as it had been for Jillian. Strange that neither seemed aware of the other's suffering.

Two hours later, most of the boys had left and Russ had given the reporter all the information he could about the project. As camera equipment was knocked down and packed up, the reporter scanned the gym.

"What happened to the woman who was here earlier?" The question sounded just a bit too casual.

As the group of young people was starting to thin, Russ had noticed that Audrey made herself scarce, too. "I'm not sure. People drift in and out."

"Isn't she . . ."

Russ pretended not to hear. He extended a hand to the reporter and sidestepped the question he didn't want to hear. "Listen, if I can do anything else for you, give me a call at the station."

"Sure." The reporter shook his hand. But the end of the conversation didn't end his speculation, Russ could tell from the look on his face. "I'll be in touch. I have a hunch I'll be needing more information."

RUSS RESTED HIS FACE against Jillian's stomach. She sat propped against the pillows in his bed, feeding him bites of frozen yogurt.

"Mother enjoyed the Youth Center yesterday," she told him. He raised himself up enough to close his lips over her nipple.

"I don't want to talk about your mother," he murmured.

"Watch out, or I'll sit this bowl in your lap."

"You wouldn't dare."

"Dares are dangerous. Don't you know—"

The telephone rang.

"Saved by the bell," he whispered as she reached for the phone on his bedside table.

"Mr. Flynn's personal assistant," she said in the sultriest voice he'd ever heard. As payback, he buried his tongue in her navel. She giggled as she handed him the phone. "Oh, Mr. Flynn, you're too kind."

"Flynn here."

"Must be true." Ron chuckled at the other end of the line.

"What's that?" Russ asked his sportscaster friend.

"It's right here on the news wire, pal."

Russ struggled to sit up. "What is?"

"Story just moved on the wire, my man. Comedian Audrey Tate is leaving her fifth husband—and the most likely reason is her young lover, Florida disc jockey Russ Flynn."

12

THE NEXT MORNING Jillian's response to the revelation that her mother and Russ were making headlines was typical: she packed her bags.

She was shoving a drawer noisily shut when Audrey stuck her head around the bedroom door, rubbing sleep-bleary eyes.

"Goodness gracious, what on earth are you doing?" She stared at the open canvas bag, then leaned closer to the digital clock on Jillian's bedside table. "Do you have any idea what time it is, Jillie? It's only four-twelve in the morning. What are you doing up at this ungodly hour?"

Jillian didn't even look up. She zipped the bag in one swift movement and slipped the strap over her shoulder. "I'm going to work, Mother. Then I'm leaving town for the weekend."

Audrey plopped onto the unmade bed, looking less perturbed at Jillian's announcement than she had looked upon realizing she was up before dawn. She yawned deeply and leaned back against a pillow. "Well, have a nice time, lovey."

Her mother's blithe attitude was the last straw. With a violent heave, Jillian threw her just-packed bag against the headboard, mere inches from Audrey's engagingly tousled hair. Audrey's eyes shot open. "What in the—"

"Doesn't anything faze you?" Jillian took two steps in Audrey's direction, then halted. Now that she'd unleashed the anger that had kept her up all night, she was afraid she would totally lose control. "Doesn't anything ever make you want to shout, 'Enough!'?"

For once, Audrey looked speechless. "Why—I— Whatever are you talking about?"

"I'm talking about Russ! I'm talking about my life!" Jillian flailed her arms in the air. "I'm talking about the way you keep turning up and ruining my life!"

Jillian heard her mother gasp behind her. Her outburst had dissipated her anger as had the bewildered reaction of Audrey, who truly didn't understand the damage that had been done.

"Why, Jillie. Do I do that?"

Jillian closed her eyes. She had to leave. She had to be at the station in half an hour. She had to go on the air and be funny and coherent and entertaining. But first, she had to resolve this ugly scene she'd started.

Her voice calmed, she turned to face Audrey. "Yes, Mother. You do. You always have."

"Always?"

"Always, Mother."

Audrey straightened, squaring her shoulders, and studied her daughter for a long time. "Well, it was certainly foolish of you to wait all this time to tell me. Now, wasn't it?"

Jillian smiled—a weak, nearly defeated smile. Confrontations seldom worked with Audrey, who simply retreated behind whatever would make the unpleasantness disappear most quickly. But Jillian had said what she needed to say. The moment's anger, at least, had been lanced and would no longer fester inside her.

But the anger's dissipation left room for something else she had been able to ignore—a terrible emptiness at the center of her soul.

AFTER SHE SIGNED OFF, Jillian took step two in her weekend-escape plan—she arranged to borrow Rosa's boat.

And Rosa's advice was hauntingly familiar.

"Running away won't solve anything," Rosa said as she wrote down directions to the boat, docked at Shell Point on the Gulf Coast.

"I know." Jillian dropped the keys into the pocket of her leather skirt, then folded up the sheet of directions, pretending her hands didn't tremble. She was no longer angry, but she was far from being as cool as she wanted to appear. Right now, she was frightened. Frightened of the loneliness that was certain to return when Russ left her life. Frightened of seeing her life turned into a public spectacle once again. Frightened of seeing the satisfaction in Jim Towers's eyes as he anticipated the ratings value of her unhappiness. She smiled blandly to hide her fear. "Running may not help, but I'm so good at it. I've been doing it all my life. Why change now?"

"Because eventually it helps to grow up?"

"Face the music and all that jazz?"

"You got it. Unless you're too big a chicken."

Jillian stared at her new friend. "You don't let up, do you?"

Rosa shook her head.

"All right." She picked up the phone on Rosa's desk and started dialing. What difference could it possibly make, anyway? She'd already started sending out résumés, making calls. Something would turn up. It always did. Then none of this would matter. "I'll face the music. *Then* I'll run."

Rosa sat down and propped her feet up on her desk. "This should be interesting."

It took about two minutes to get the reporter from the *Tallahassee Democrat* on the line—two minutes during which Jillian was sorely tempted to hang up and continue with Plan A. But Rosa's skeptical smirk kept her hanging on the line.

She introduced herself to the reporter, feeling as if she were watching from a distance. Surely she wasn't doing this.

"Anyway, I wanted you to know that Russ Flynn isn't Audrey Tate's lover." She was unable to smile at the astonished look on Rosa's face, but only because she couldn't really believe she was doing this. "He's *my* lover. And Audrey Tate is my mother."

The reporter burst into a barrage of questions, but Jillian didn't even listen to them. "I'm sorry, that's the only comment I have. But you're free to print it. And if you'd like to confirm it, I have the station's public-relations director right here."

She handed the receiver to Rosa. "Now it's your problem."

Then she walked out and drove home.

She made the half-hour drive to Shell Point wrapped in a mental fog. Audrey had protested all the while she'd packed, promising to clear things up, but Jillian had ignored her, too. "It's too late to clear things up, Mother."

"But Russ—"

"Forget about Russ, Mother. *I'm* going to."

She wondered, as the Spanish moss-draped oaks lining the highway reminded her of Russ's place in the country, if she could forget about Russ. Forget his touch? Forget the understanding in his eyes? Forget the way he brought her alive as no one ever had?

Tears stung her eyes and trickled down her cheeks.

Dammit! She wiped at the dampness with the back of her hand. *You never cry. Never! So just stop it. Now!*

She tried concentrating, instead, on how angry she was with Audrey for ruining things again. But she discovered that she couldn't seem to dump it in Audrey's lap anymore; and it didn't keep her mind off Russ, anyway.

Catching sight of the wooded cove at Shell Point where Rosa docked her thirty-five-footer, *The Biggest Toy,* gave Jillian a lift. The water glistened in the sunlight. Soon she would be on the water. Alone. Beyond reach.

She drove into the numbered parking space and grabbed her overnight bag from the seat beside her. There it was—*The Biggest Toy.* White and sleek and her ticket to escape.

Jillian didn't even bother to go below deck. As quickly as possible, she familiarized herself with the boat's operation and pulled away from its slip. The engine chugged, the water churned quietly around her. She glanced over her shoulder as the land grew farther away.

"You can't get me now," she muttered at the invisible demons that had followed her so much of her life. "I'm out of reach—for two days, anyway."

She maneuvered the unfamiliar waters carefully, guiding the boat through the narrow opening of the cove and out into the Gulf. *The Biggest Toy* was larger than anything she'd operated before, but she was confident she could handle it. That confidence grew as the Gulf spread out before her, calm and brilliant in the May sunshine.

The soothing effects of the water and the solitude were just taking effect when she heard a movement behind her. Turning to see if something had shifted or fallen, she was startled and dismayed to see a broadly smiling face peering up from below.

"Ship's crew reporting for duty, Captain." Russ stepped out onto the deck and saluted smartly.

"No!" Jillian's hands tightened into white-knuckle fists. "I won't have it. You can't do this to me, Russ Flynn."

He moved toward the bow to stand beside her. He placed a hand at the small of her back and ignored it when she tensed and pulled away from his touch.

"I'm here to help, Captain."

"I'm perfectly capable of handling this boat alone." She checked her instruments and prepared to turn back toward land.

"Sure, the boat. Handling the boat's easy. Although I do think Rosa felt more comfortable knowing I'd be here to lend a hand."

Rosa. The traitor. Jillian vowed to get even. Soon.

"But, Jillie, what about the moonlight on the water? You can't possibly expect to handle that alone—that's clearly a job for two." The tone of his voice told her he had no intention of letting her lapse into a serious discussion. "Surely you can see that. And what about the wind in your face? Who's going to taste your lips and make sure it's genuine salt air and not some cheap imitation?"

"I'm heading back."

He reached out to take over the boat's controls. "No, you're not."

Fury—hot, frustrated, blind—flooded her at the show of physical strength she couldn't hope to match.

"Dammit, Russ! Get away from me. Get off this boat. Get out of my life!"

"And toss away a weekend on the water with the sexiest number I know? Not a chance."

"What do you want from me? My pride? You've got that and more, thanks to your damn headlines." She turned to face him. "My job? Take that, too, if you want it. Just take it and leave me alone!"

Easing up on the throttle, Russ turned to her. She tried to twist away from his gaze, but he captured her face in his hands and forced her to look at him.

"What do I want from you?" All the teasing had gone out of his voice, and was replaced by a desperate intensity. "The one thing you've never learned how to give, apparently. To hell with your pride. That's always going to get trampled, one way or another. We both know that. And screw your job. I've got one of my own that I don't even want anymore."

He stopped, his hands tightening on her face. He leaned closer and lightly touched his lips to hers. "All I want from you is your love, Jillie. You've already got mine. Seems like a fair trade-off to me."

Her throat tightened and she swallowed hard. "It's not that easy, Russ."

"It is if you let it be."

"It isn't." She blinked against the tears. "I may love you, but—"

"*May* love me? Is that the best you can do?"

She looked up into his face. He was determined to have it—the declaration she so wanted to avoid. At the look on his face, the words welled up in her, filling her, making it impossible for her to hold it in.

"I do love you." But the words were spoken with more dismay than joy.

He gathered her gently into his arms. She felt the strength there—a strength that went beyond the firm muscles in his arms; a strength rooted somewhere deep inside him that enfolded her.

But the idea of trusting that strength frightened her. It couldn't really hold up against the kind of turmoil Audrey's presence had already visited upon them—and no doubt would again, if they tried to build a normal life. Even love couldn't be strong enough to stand up to that. Could it?

"If you love me, everything else is easy."

"You don't know."

He kissed the top of her head. "Jillie, you're not a little girl anymore. Nobody's going to laugh at you now. No more fractured nursery rhymes on the playground."

"And no more supermarket-tabloid headlines?" She buried her face in his soft cotton shirt, squeezing her eyes shut at the image. "No more leers when I walk down the street? Can you promise me that?"

He was silent for too long. She listened to his heart pounding.

"No. I can't promise you that. All I can promise is that I'll be there. I'll hold your hand. I'll be at your side."

"And that will make it all better?" She made the words sound skeptical, bitter. But deep in her heart, she was starting to believe them herself.

"Yes. If you allow it."

She listened to the water lap against the side of the boat, to the reassuring beat of his heart beneath her ear.

Maybe he was right.

JILLIAN LAY ON DECK, her eyes closed, the wind ruffling her hair, while Russ massaged sunscreen into her tense shoulders, her back, her legs.

"That's dangerous territory," she murmured with a soft, appreciative growl as he smoothed lotion along the insides of her thighs.

"You're telling me." He slowed the motion to a sensual crawl. "I don't suppose you'd be agreeable to finishing this job below deck?"

"I wouldn't need the sunscreen below deck." She propped her head on her elbow and grinned at him.

"Are you being thickheaded or just stubborn?"

She rolled back onto her stomach. "Just stubborn. Now, finish the job."

He trickled lotion along the back of her other leg. "Bet I can hold out longer than you can."

She grunted her doubt. "Not in those swim trunks, you can't. They weren't built to take the pressure."

"Now who's evil?"

"So it's contagious. You have only yourself to blame."

But he fooled her. By the time he finished covering her with sunscreen, the sun seemed distinctly hotter on her flesh. And by the time he finished massaging her feet—"They deserve it, after what you make them suffer through"—the tingling had moved up to her calves and on to her thighs.

"You're not playing fair," she whispered.

"I don't know what you're talking about." He leaned down to brush a kiss over the small of her back.

Jillian felt the sweet, familiar tightening deep inside that couldn't be denied. "I'm warning you. If you don't play fair, you'll live to regret it. I'll make you my love slave."

"You've got that backward, Jillie. I'm making *you* my love slave."

He laughed at her playfully wide-eyed look of horror. She jumped up and started toward him. "You've gone too far now, Flynn."

"I was hoping you'd say that." He laughed, moving toward the short ladder leading below deck.

She stalked him, as slowly and threateningly as she could manage on the gently rocking boat—across the deck and down the ladder, until she cornered him in the bedroom.

She laughed and stepped forward, her playful mood evaporating as soon as she felt his arms close around her. "It will be all right, won't it?"

"How much worse can it get?" He kissed her closed eyelids. "They've got me sleeping with your mother. If we can survive that, they can't do anything to hurt us. Right?"

"Right."

His confidence in the strength of a love that still felt fragile and uncertain filled Jillian's heart. They undressed slowly and lay down on the bed. And for the first time, their mating was more emotion than passion. When Russ entered her, Jillian knew this union was much more than a physical one. And when they rocked together, shaken and moved by the same waves of pleasure, Jillian felt her love grow stronger.

But as the waves subsided, she still wondered if it was strong enough to see her through whatever might come after the weekend.

THEY ATE AND SUNNED and slept and made love. But as Sunday afternoon ticked away and they headed back to Shell Point, Russ could sense Jillian becoming tense again.

"Do we have to go back?" she asked, smiling weakly as they secured the boat and packed up their gear.

"We could elope."

"That's my specialty, you know. Running away."

He hated the sound of defeat taking hold in her voice. He wanted to shake her up, tell her that his love was powerful enough to get them through a few days of adverse publicity. "At least if we eloped, we'd be running *to* something, not just *away* from something."

When he informed her that he had come down on his motorcycle and they wouldn't be able to make the ride back together, Jillian's face grew even more dismayed.

"Don't worry. I'll be right behind you," he promised, pulling his helmet on as she prepared to drive away.

But her backward glance in the rearview mirror was wistful. The idyllic weekend had ended entirely too quickly for Russ, too. He patted himself on the back for calling Rosa when he hadn't been able to get Jillian on the phone. Despite that damned reporter's insistence, Russ had found it hard to believe that Jillian had called to tell the newspaper they were lovers. But it all added up when Rosa explained what had happened. Thank goodness he'd just hopped on the bike and followed Jillian. If he hadn't pulled a fast one on her, she would have spent the entire weekend brooding.

He hoped she hadn't done just that all the way back to Tallahassee—brooded herself into one of her moods. If so, he told himself when he turned into the condo parking lot, he would just have to coax her out of it again.

Then he saw the trucks. The equipment. The small band of high-tech vultures lounging under the palm trees at the edge of the parking lot.

The media had descended. And they were waiting to pick Jillian's bones.

He roared into his parking space, but Jillian hadn't waited for him. Her face a frozen mask, she was already shouldering her way through the crowd by the time he got off his bike. As he made his way in her direction, he heard the questions they were shouting at her.

"J.T., is it true about your affair with your mother's lover?"

"Miss Joyner, would you like to comment on the stories that you and your mother are sharing the affections of your competitor?"

"J.T., I understand you introduced Audrey and this Flynn fellow. Is that true?"

He cringed, knowing how the inevitable barrage of questions was piercing through her. Each question shamed her, angered her, resurrected her conviction that she didn't stand a chance of a normal life. When he caught up with her and tried to bolster her by putting his arm around her shoulder, she didn't even look up.

"Is this Flynn?"

The questions continued to come, too fast for answers.

"Mr. Flynn, do you love either woman? Or is this just . . ."

"Russ, what's it like to be with both . . ."

He wanted to punch someone. All of them. He'd never felt such rage. A thousand denials leaped to his lips but he forced himself to swallow them. Whatever he said, he knew instinctively, wouldn't be the right thing; wouldn't sound the way he'd intended when it came out in tomorrow's paper or on tonight's news.

But the fury boiling in him was almost more than he could contain—because he knew that every word was driving Jillian deeper into her shell, wedging her further away from him, destroying every bit of the wonderful intimacy they had nurtured this weekend.

The media were killing his chances with Jillian.

And he wanted to kill one of them—all of them—for what they were doing. He wanted to kill them on behalf of Jillian, who had learned far too early just how cruel the world can be when it's hungry for gossip.

Yet Russ squelched his impulse, buried it, just the way Jillian was burying her burning emotions. Because for him to do anything else would simply hurt her more. And that was the one thing he wouldn't do—even for the satisfaction of smashing in a face or two.

After what seemed interminable moments spent covering the short distance to her front door, they squeezed into her condo without saying a word.

Audrey's breezy smile greeted them. "I'm so glad you two are back. Isn't this terrible?"

Russ wondered if she was as unconcerned as she sounded. "Has it been like this all weekend?"

"Mostly, I suppose." Audrey walked back to the couch to retrieve her brandy. "Would you like a drink? No? I tried to talk to them at first, but they just weren't listening. They've got this crazy idea in their heads—and when they think they've sniffed out a hot story they really don't want to hear anything else. Jillie, are you all right? You look pale, lovey."

Russ stared at Audrey, wondering if she could truly be as oblivious as she appeared to what her daughter was going through—had gone through all her life. Suddenly he was furious at Audrey, too. She might be adorable. She might even be so naive that some of her actions were understandable. But one fact remained: She was a grown woman who was insensitive to her daughter's pain.

Jillian's strained bubble of laughter drew his attention.

"I'm fine, Mother. Just fine. Any reason why I shouldn't be?"

"Well, I realize all these press people . . ."

Increasingly impatient with Audrey's offhand attitude, Russ took one of Jillian's hands in his. "It won't be like this anymore, Jillian. You have to trust me on that. We'll call Rosa and she and I will straighten everything out, and—"

Jillian jerked her hand out of his. "And life will be just rosy. Is that it, Russ? A real fairy tale, starring the princess daughter of the queen of Hollywood, complete with a happily-ever-after ending."

"You and I can have a normal life." Russ heard the pleading in his voice—a pleading that grew out of the fear that he wouldn't be able to convince her. "It doesn't have to be this way."

"I'll never have a normal life!" She pointed to Audrey. "Thanks to her, I'll never have a normal life!"

Against her will, he gripped her shoulders and compelled her to look him in the eye. "You're the one who decides that, Jillian. Not her. You *are* her daughter. Learn to live with it. As long as you try to pretend you're not

Audrey Tate's daughter, you're right—you never will have a normal life. You'll always be on the run."

Jillian stared at him in silence, then raised her arms to break his hold on her. Her voice held a deadly chill when she spoke. "You may be right, Russ. You may have this all figured out. I may be doing this to myself. But I can tell you one thing: I won't be responsible for doing it to anyone else. I won't bring another generation into the world to have their childhood stolen from them the way mine was. I won't."

She whirled and dashed into her bedroom, slamming the door behind her. Before he had taken two steps in her direction, Russ heard the lock click into place.

"Goodness, she is in a snit, isn't she?" Audrey's voice was only mildly incredulous. "And I know she blames me for all this."

Russ stared at the woman who was to blame and who wasn't to blame. She'd had no more of a childhood than Jillian, he was certain, having been raised the daughter of a vaudeville star. But where Audrey had blossomed under the attention, Jillian had shriveled. How could immature, self-centered Audrey be expected to know that her shy, sensitive daughter couldn't revel in the attention as she had?

And how could he ever hope to convince Jillian that life wouldn't always be the kind of widely publicized fiasco she'd always experienced? If the truth were told, he wasn't sure himself.

13

RUSS TRIED TO BE AMUSED by the strange looks he received from everyone at WKIX Monday morning. Some were amused, some knowing, some shocked. Some people avoided looking, or coming near him altogether.

He was bothered by how the people he couldn't see—his listeners—were reacting to the news. He had to admit, the twisted stories made him sound more than a little depraved. So it didn't surprise him that some who called while he was on the air wanted to know the real story.

"Say, Russ, what's the scoop, pal?" asked one of his regular callers, after winning the daily trivia quiz. "Sounds like your love life has really picked up."

At that moment, Russ knew, every WKIX listener would have reached over to turn up the volume to be sure to catch what came next. But his mind was blank. He had no answer.

"Reports of my harem are greatly exaggerated," he said finally, hoping none of his listeners heard the strain in his voice.

But the denials didn't help. Almost everyone who called that morning wanted to know more—everyone except Howie, who called right after Russ went off the air.

Russ was instantly alert. None of the kids from the center had ever called him at the station. "Hey, what's up?" he asked Howie.

"Just wanted to let you know, they picked my mom up last week. The police. She had— She was with some people dealing drugs. And . . . I guess she's been doing 'em, too."

Russ dropped into a chair. Suddenly, a little publicity about his love life didn't seem quite so important. "Sorry, man. What can I do?"

"Nothing, I guess." Howie sounded even younger and more unsure of himself than usual. "But she feels really bad about everything, Russ. They put her in a rehab program. She said everything'll be different now."

"Maybe she's right."

"Sure. Now she'll get straight and won't be taking off all the time. Right?"

Russ did all he could to reassure Howie, promising to meet him at the center by midafternoon. Then, almost before he returned the phone to its cradle, one of the clerks stuck his head into the room.

"Tony wants to see you, Flynn."

The last thing Russ wanted to deal with this morning was his station manager. But he got up from the chair and went down the hall to Tony Covington's office.

Tony, he discovered, was one of the ones who wouldn't look him in the eye. Not a good sign, Russ decided. Tony had always looked him in the eye, even when he was in a real stew over something.

"You got anything to say for yourself?" No preamble, just brusque and to the point.

"You want an excuse from my mother?" Russ coached himself not to be testy, but he wasn't sure it was working. "'Please excuse Russ today, he fell in love.'"

"You fell in love?" Tony's voice oozed sarcasm. "With which one, lover boy?"

Astounded that anyone who knew him would believe the wild rumors being circulated, Russ clamped his jaw shut. It was a matter of self-preservation. He hadn't slugged any of the vultures yesterday, but if Tony pushed him too far, he might just take a pop at him. He was primed for it.

"Listen, pal, who you sleep with isn't usually my business." Now Tony looked him straight in the eye. "But this time it is. I told you to stay away from that woman and keep your mind on your work. You didn't do it and you see where it got us."

"The publicity will blow over, Tony. You know that." Russ spat the words out as calmly as he could.

"It's not the publicity I'm worried about, dammit! It's the ratings. They're down. Way down."

Russ was silent in the hope that Tony would cool down. He squelched the urge to defend himself. But he was unprepared for the words that came next.

"We think it's time for a change, Flynn."

"What are you talking about?" But he didn't really have to ask. He knew. Every on-air personality knew what those words meant. He felt queasy.

"Your contract runs out the end of this month. The station thinks it best if we don't renew."

After that, his audience with the station manager ended quickly. Dazed, Russ didn't even go back to the production room to work up promos for the next day's program. He walked out to the parking lot, got on his motorcycle and rode off.

He began to recognize the queasy feeling. *Fear.* Fear that he wouldn't survive. Fear that he didn't have anything to offer the world but his talent for talking trash on the air. And he knew now what Jillian had known most of her life—exposing yourself to the mercy of the public was one helluva scary way to lead your life.

Jillian. He wanted to see Jillian. Had to see her. She would understand. And he had to make her understand that he now understood. Because they had to work this out. If no other good came out of this rotten mess, at least it had brought Jillian into his life.

He'd rather lose a thousand jobs than lose Jillian, he told himself as he pulled into the WFLA parking lot. But losing the job was still tough to swallow—especially right now, when he felt close to losing Jillian, too.

Before Russ could find Jillian, a wiry, intense-looking man flawlessly turned out in a double-breasted suit cornered him in one of the narrow corridors.

"We haven't met yet, but we spoke a few months back. I'm Jim Towers."

Russ recognized the station manager's name. He was struck by the strong hunch that this crisp, contained guy would never lose his cool the way Tony Covington did. It wasn't a reassuring thought, however.

"Do you have a few minutes?" Towers gestured to an open office door.

"Actually, I—"

"Five minutes should do it."

And Russ found himself in the uncluttered, carefully maintained office, sitting across the desk from Jim Towers, who smiled placidly and confidently at him.

"I have a proposition for you, Flynn. One I think you'll find quite attractive."

Russ shifted uncomfortably in the chair. This conversation was no more welcome than the last one he'd had in a station manager's office. He knew it made him crazy, but the last thing he wanted from Jim Towers was a job offer.

"I'm really not interested in—"

"My sources tell me you should be interested, Flynn. I want you in the morning slot here at 'FLA. With J.T." The barest of smiles twitched the corners of his mustache. "I think you'll make a very appealing team."

Before Russ could respond, the door behind him opened. Towers's face barely changed expression. "J.T., I'm so glad you could join us. Mr. Flynn and I were just discussing the possibility of a little teamwork. You two would make an intriguing morning duo, don't you agree?"

Russ opened his mouth as Jillian swept into the room. She turned to Russ, her green eyes narrowed and suspicious.

"I don't work as a team. Not with him."

"How uncharitable of you. Unfortunately, Mr. Flynn will be out of work by the end of the month. This seemed an excellent solution to his dilemma."

Russ saw the split second of shock, followed by hesitation in Jillian's eyes. "Is that true?"

"It is, but . . ."

She turned to Towers. "Then put *him* on the air. I'll go somewhere else. I think it's time for me to move on, anyway."

"I'm not interested in Flynn alone, J.T. After all, his popularity is in a slide. But with you at his side . . ."

Towers let the words hang. Before Russ could open his mouth, Jillian stalked out of the office.

"Don't worry about her," Towers said. "She'll come around. Now—"

But Russ was already rising from his seat. "Thanks, Towers, but I've got a few other things on the line."

It was only a half lie anyway, he told himself as he chased Jillian down the hall. He had been looking halfheartedly for something else. Now he would just look wholeheartedly.

He caught up with her at the door to the employees' lounge. "Jillian, we have to talk."

Her anger was evident in the set of her chin, but so was her confusion and uncertainty. "I can't believe you were plotting with him behind my back."

"That's not what was happening in there. I came here looking for you."

"And just happened to fall into a pleasant little tête-à-tête with Towers?"

"Dammit, Jillian. This morning's been lousy enough without you getting on my case."

She seemed to soften. "Is it true? You're out at 'KIX?"

"Yeah. It's true."

She sighed and put a hand on his arm. "I'm sorry, Russ."

"But I'm not interested in Towers's offer. You have to know that."

"Sure. I . . . I understand."

But he understood the look in her eyes, too. The look that said she held herself responsible for ruining his career—and salvaging it.

He tried to reassure her. "I'll land on my feet. I always do."

He only hoped that was true.

THE HORDE OUTSIDE HER front door had diminished somewhat by the time Jillian reached home Monday afternoon, although a few reporters still lingered in anticipation of catching a glimpse of Audrey Tate and company.

The reporters didn't surprise her. The sight of her mother's packed bags by the front door did.

"I'm leaving," Audrey announced, glancing in the mirror to check the details of her outfit. "I will be so glad to get out of this humidity. I don't see how you stand it."

The strangest feeling flooded Jillian. The anger was gone. The bitterness was at bay, at least for the moment. She felt abandoned and alone and, yes, almost sad. Not because her mother was leaving, but because once again they hadn't been able to get beyond the surface of their relationship. Once again, they hadn't been able to reach an understanding about how very different they were— and decide it didn't matter. "Your agent isn't expecting you in Hollywood to sign the contract until next week. Where are you going?"

Audrey shrugged with elaborate unconcern. "Home."

"Home?"

"I called Henry today. I've decided not to take that silly movie role. Something else will come along."

Jillian gave her mother an awkward hug. "I'm glad."

"So am I, Jillie. So am I." She sighed deeply and Jillian noticed, for the first time, that the sparkle was dimmer in her mother's emerald eyes. "I'm tired of all this hoopla. I don't think I knew how tired until this weekend, until . . ."

Jillian wanted to hear it. She wanted to hear her mother say something that wasn't superficial and shallow. "Until what?"

The touch of Audrey's hand on her cheek was unexpected, and it, too, stirred feelings that were hard to label.

"Until I saw the way it tore your life in two, Jillie. Until I started thinking about how many other times..." She paused to compose herself. "This isn't the first time, is it? It's just the first time I've noticed."

Jillian smiled. It was easier, somehow, to smile armed with the knowledge that at last someone understood. "Not the first. Probably not the last, either."

Audrey cocked a carefully drawn eyebrow. "Now, Jillie, don't be cynical. Anyway, I've grown quite weary of all the fuss and bother. Henry's a good man. I think I'd just like to enjoy some time with him."

Jillian hoped that was true. Perhaps something good had come out of this whole mess, after all.

Audrey reached out to smooth a carefully moussed curl away from Jillian's eyes. *A mother's gesture*, Jillian thought.

"After all, when you find a good man, you have to be careful to hold on to him." Audrey lapsed into the role of dispenser of maternal wisdom. "You have no idea how difficult it can be to find a good man. It's taken me five tries, you know. Five *official* tries, that is."

"That's good advice, Mother. I'll keep it in mind." Despite the deep well of hurt that her mother's words tapped, Jillian couldn't help but smile. Audrey Tate giving advice on men?

"See that you do, lovey." She picked up her French-tapestry garment bag and matching duffel. "My cab should be here any moment. Do you suppose one of those nice TV fellows would carry these out to the front for me? I wouldn't mind having a few words with them before I go."

"You've got to be kidding."

"No. I think the world deserves to know that I'm placing love before my career." She paused with her hand on the doorknob. "Don't you think that will make a nice story?"

Then she was out the door. And soon the whirlwind that accompanied her would subside, as it always did. Jillian only wished the havoc left in its wake would vanish as quickly.

But it wouldn't. She knew that from experience.

"For now, you've got your own packing to do," she told herself, surprised at the weariness in her voice.

She had spent the afternoon on the phone and she'd finally hit pay dirt. One of her former colleagues in Atlanta had put her on to a station in Kansas that had an opening. A hurry-up interview had been arranged for the next afternoon. From the pocket of her leather skirt, Jillian pulled the ticket she'd picked up from a travel agent near the station and tossed it onto the coffee table. Time to perfect the Jammin' J.T. image for tomorrow.

She combed through her closet, bored with the prospect. She would have to give her very best performance. Her heart might not be in it, but it was the only solution she could think of that would restore Russ's career.

And surely, in Kansas, she might find the anonymity she'd been seeking for so long.

Three outfits were spread on the bed when the doorbell rang. Worried it might be one of the reporters, she tiptoed quietly to the door and peered through the peephole. It was Russ.

Perversely, she wanted to see him—wanted to reassure herself that he would be all right, that he hadn't given up, that he would still be smiling his larger-than-life smile from billboards all over the Florida panhandle long after the Tallahassee Lassie had been forgotten.

She opened the door, feeling an odd mixture of relief and sadness.

"I don't even know what to say." He moved into the room, hands shoved deeply into his jeans pockets.

"I know," she admitted. "How'd your day go? It just doesn't have the right ring to it."

He nodded and sat on the couch. "I suppose we're safe in assuming that neither one of us had a great day."

She sat in a nearby chair. She wanted to brush the weariness off his face, erase the lines of tension at the corners of his always smiling mouth—almost always smiling mouth. Sometimes it was otherwise occupied. She tried not to remember.

"I just wanted to make sure you understood that I wouldn't take the job at 'FLA if Towers offered it," he announced in a rush.

He was as uncomfortable as she was. She would have time to mourn the loss of their intimacy later. Later, when she was a stranger in Kansas.

"Things will work out," she told him. She just didn't tell him how they would work out. He would find out soon enough.

"We'll work them out together." The flatness suddenly left his voice. It grew intense, to match the sudden determination in his face.

She looked away.

"What's this?" He had the airline ticket in his hand. "Is Audrey leaving?"

"No, she's already—" She stopped herself. "I mean, yes. She's leaving. She's going home."

Russ studied the ticket. "To Kansas?"

Jillian slumped back in the armchair. "Why don't you drop it, Russ?"

"Audrey's already gone, isn't she? This is your ticket, isn't it?"

She didn't answer. There was no reason to answer; he already knew.

"What's in Kansas, Jillian? Another job? Another place to run to? A fresh start, where nobody knows you and you can hide again?"

She wasn't even angry. She didn't have the energy for it. Besides, it wouldn't be anger that overwhelmed her; it would be the anguish of losing him.

"That's right, Russ. Another job. Tallahassee is all yours again."

Russ jumped up and knelt before her, placing his hands on her knees. "You can't do this. I won't allow you to do this."

"It isn't your choice."

"The hell, it isn't. I'll follow you. I'll get Towers to sue you for running out on your contract. I'll—"

"You've leave me alone and get on with your life," she said, tensing her knees against the sensations that arose at his touch. "That's what you'll do, Russ Flynn."

"Jillian, you can't spend the rest of your life running."

She smiled. "If I run far enough, eventually I'll leave it all behind me. I deserve the chance to do that."

Even as she said it, she didn't believe it.

"You'll never leave it behind. Don't you see that? It's inside you. And you'll never divide your life into two safe, separate compartments. Don't you see? Right now you're more crippled by trying to hide from publicity— by trying to hide from life—than you would be by the publicity itself."

His words zinged through her consciousness, striking a chord. *Damn him for making it all so complicated!*

She stood abruptly, leaving him on his knees in front of her chair. "I have things to take care of now, Russ. And we both have to get up early tomorrow. Maybe you should go."

He slumped for a moment, then stood and walked over to her. Before she knew what was happening, he pulled her to him and crushed her lips under his in a bruising, demanding kiss. His mouth moved over hers angrily, insistently, telling her of all his hurt and frustration. His feelings poured into her, filling her with the need to heal his hurts—and her own.

But he ended the kiss abruptly.

"You can send me away. You can even run away yourself. But you'll never be rid of me, Jillian. Just like I'll never be rid of you."

14

"DULL, DULL, DULL," Jillian muttered, peering into the bowl of cream-of-asparagus soup.

The soup was dull. The routine she'd been working on all afternoon for tomorrow's program was dull. Even the clothes she'd hung on the closet door—a body-skimming royal blue number that she'd always felt sensational in before—struck her as dull.

What she needed, she told herself as she moved the bowl of soup into the sink, uneaten, was a change. And the change would come soon.

Not soon, she chided herself. Tomorrow morning. As soon as she returned the message to the station manager in Kansas.

"J.T., let's get down to business," the confident Midwestern voice on her answering machine had said when she got home that afternoon. "We want you to pack your bags for Kansas. Give me a call when you get in."

She should have called back before now. She'd meant to. It wasn't as if the station manager's call was a surprise. She knew she'd impressed the people at the station in Kansas. And they had a slot to fill right away. She'd expected to hear from them before the week was out. And she would call them. Tomorrow. Early tomorrow.

And that'll be dull, too, a tiny voice whispered in her ear as she settled into her armchair. Because life was dull. Empty. Vacant. Like a quiet death stealing over her. But even "dull" beat the anguish lurking below the surface, waiting to rear its ugly face at the first opportunity.

"You know what's wrong, don't you?" Rosa had asked while they lounged by the pool the afternoon before.

"Stomach virus," Jillian had replied. Rosa had merely snorted in response.

Jillian didn't need Rosa to tell her what was wrong. She missed Russ. At first, he had simply haunted her—all the way to Kansas and back—with his words of warning. But he was wrong, dammit. She *could* keep her private life private and still enjoy the part of her that loved to perform.

She *could*. She *would*. She would show him.

Except, of course, he wasn't here to see.

She looked down at her notes for the routine she wanted to do on the legislative proposal to raise taxes.

Even you *aren't interested in it*, she chided herself. *Do you really expect anybody else to be?*

Reaching for the remote control, she switched the TV on in time for the local evening news. Surely the news would give her some ideas for tomorrow's show—unless her mind was growing as dull as everything else in her life.

There'd been a breakthrough in the serial murder case. Definitely not material for a humorous skit. Gasoline prices up. Housing prices down. Those topics had already been done—by her and everyone else. She yawned.

Just as a matter of curiosity, she'd listened to Russ this morning. Just to see what he was using—no other reason. He was funny. As funny as ever. Obviously, he wasn't suffering from the blahs that had settled over her life. Obviously, Russ Flynn was fine.

His voice had been cheerful. She could see the smile that went with it when he spoke. "And now, for our Christmas-in-July contest, we're... What's that?" He'd paused. "Oh. It's not even July. May. It's May. And we can't do Christmas in May. Has no pizzazz. Fine. Mind if I just sign off now?"

Then he'd turned the tables on the people who traditionally came to Florida for the winter months, speculating that Floridians should head north to get away from the humidity for the summer.

Jillian had actually laughed. She'd even reached for the phone, to tell him how much she'd enjoyed it. Then she remembered. It was over. This whole episode would be over soon. As soon as she returned the call from Kansas.

Jillian concentrated on the TV news again.

A tawny young face, dimpled just at the left-hand corner of the mouth and wearing a crystal earring, filled the screen. The face looked familiar, but Jillian couldn't place it. No reason she should recognize it, but she edged the volume up anyway.

"My mom's gonna be gone for a while, with a rehab program," he was saying, hesitantly but almost proudly. "She's gonna get straightened out. Then things'll be different."

They cut to a noisy gymnasium, where the teen was part of a group playing basketball. Now Jillian recognized the boy. He was one of the Youth Power kids she'd met at FSU. She listened intently to the voice-over.

"Thanks to the success of the program for young people like Howie, Youth Power will become a permanently funded part of the Leon County schools next year," the modulated voice said accompanied by the background sound of shoes squeaking and the thud of a basketball. "Heading up the program will be a man with a familiar face in Tallahassee and at the Youth Center where the program has been based—Russ Flynn, who will end his career with WKIX radio to oversee the program."

Jillian's heart lurched. Russ's wide smile seemed directed at her. So did the tired eyes. Especially the tired eyes.

"I'm not moving into this spot because I'm a genius at working with kids," Russ said. "But I know where they're coming from—my mother would be the first to tell you how much trouble they had keeping me in high school. And I think I can help the program keep the high profile, the good visibility, that will be necessary to keep it funded and successful."

The reporter then cut away from Russ to another shot of him on the basketball court with a group of teens, the voice-over telling viewers that the school board felt Russ had been more active and more successful in working with the young people than any of its other celebrity volunteers. Then the camera went back to Howie, whose young face was now serious.

"If we didn't have Russ, I don't know what some of us would do. I used to think being a teenager was, like, one of life's dirty tricks."

His earnest face brought a lump to Jillian's throat. She'd felt that way herself all too often. But she had to admit, whatever problems she'd had to deal with as a child were minor compared to what kids like Howie had to face.

The thought made her ashamed.

RUSS WAS AMAZED HOW relieved he felt each day as he signed off the air. He was ticking the days off, waiting for the time when he would be free of the pressure. Just knowing he was leaving had given back some of the pleasure he'd lost in his on-air work during the past few months.

Knowing he was leaving to work permanently with kids like Howie and André had buoyed his spirits, too. Every day, he headed out after his program, as he did now, to the Youth Center. And every day it felt more like home—more like he might be doing something worthwhile for the first time in his life.

But one emotion still overrode the rest. Actually, that wasn't quite accurate, he decided as he maneuvered his motorcycle through traffic. It was the *lack* of real emotion that overrode everything else. Because, since he'd walked out Jillian's door Monday night, knowing she was planning her escape from Tallahassee—from him—he'd been empty. No more fight, even; just emptiness.

Howie greeted him when he walked through the door. "Hey, man, did you see me on the tube last night? Was I a star, or what?"

Russ returned his exuberant smile. He hadn't seen too many smiles on Howie's face lately, and this one looked good. "You were a natural."

"Yeah. My mom saw it, too. She thought it was awesome. Said she was proud of me. Know what else she said? Said she wanted to make me that proud of her. Can you believe that? She's going to be trying real hard, she said."

Russ curbed the urge to give him a big hug. Howie wouldn't have found that awesome at all, that was certain. He slapped him on the shoulder instead. "That's great."

A chorus of catcalls and whistles from the other end of the gym diverted their attention. They turned to see Jillian, a bright blue dress clinging to her ample curves and stopping just above her shapely knees. She stood expectantly at the door of the gym.

"Man, that is one killer babe," Howie whispered.

"Yeah." Russ's heart leaped and plummeted, all at the same time. She was coming to throw herself into his arms. Or to tell him goodbye, to look her up the next time he was in Kansas. He pointed toward the other kids in the gym. "Listen, pal, do me a favor and take a hike."

But Jillian didn't head straight for him. Whatever her intention, she seemed in no hurry to carry it out. She stopped to talk to the kids. Laughing with this group. Getting a couple of the guys to show her how to execute a jump shot—an exercise that turned out to be a real attention-getter in her skyscraper heels and short dress. He even heard her delivering a slightly off-color cheer he recognized from his high-school days—a cheer that brought a loud round of laughter from the teens.

When she finally reached Russ, she wasn't laughing anymore.

"Congratulations on your new job," she said quietly.

Just being this close to her again stirred a longing in him, a longing that went far beyond physical need. He shrugged. "I told you I'd land on my feet."

"So you did."

He wished he felt as at peace with himself as she seemed.

"I've had an offer myself."

"In Kansas?"

She nodded.

"So. Congratulations are due all the way around." Maybe it would be easier this way, if she were gone, completely beyond his reach.

"You know, seeing your friend Howie on TV last night gave me a lot to think about."

He wanted to hold her. Just one more time. Wrap his arms around her and never let her go. And that, of course, was the problem. If he touched her again, he'd never give her up. And that wasn't an option.

"I realized you might be right. If I'm living in a prison, it's probably one I've built for myself." She looked down at her feet, then back up, her expression suddenly not as serene as it had been just moments before. "And I realized some prisons are worse than others. Howie's, for example. That's a tough way to live. Tougher maybe than four stepfathers."

"Don't underestimate what you've had to put up with, Jillian."

"I'm not. I'm just getting tired of letting the past rule my life."

It was small consolation at this point. Small consolation to think that some guy in Kansas might be the one to benefit from her realization. Russ just wanted this scene to be over, so he could go about the business of forgetting it. Shouldn't take more than a couple of decades, he figured, morosely.

"I talked to Rosa this morning," Jillian continued. "She seems to think that, with Jammin' J.T.'s visibility and popularity, WFLA could spearhead a volunteer mentoring program like yours—for girls. She wants Tallahassee's favorite morning DJ—now that the great Russ Flynn has retired—to kick things off, give it publicity on the air, that kind of thing. What do you think?"

"But . . . if you stay on the air, that would mean a lot of publicity. . . . You wouldn't be able to keep your private life very private anymore."

She shrugged. "I know. But I've been thinking— maybe it's time I started using my talent instead of hiding behind it. And if my position on WFLA will let me do for kids what you've been able to accomplish . . . After all, they've already accused you of having a fling with my mother. How much worse could it possibly get?"

Russ shoved his hands into his pockets—mostly to keep them from reaching for her. With that hint of vulnerability in her eyes, she looked more appealing than he'd ever seen her. But he kept his hands to himself. She'd just announced some major decisions, but none of them had anything to do with him. And he'd be damned if he was going to ask. "So, this means Kansas is out?"

"I've got better ideas than Kansas."

"Oh?"

"Yeah. I was thinking we should team up—you and I."

Team up? A thrill of hope surged in him. Hope that she wasn't talking about the same kind of teamwork her station manager had been talking about. He tested the waters. "I told you I wasn't interested in that. I like what I'm going to be doing here. I don't need radio anymore."

She moved closer. She snaked out both hands to wrap them around his neck. "I was thinking of another kind of teamwork. Something a little more . . . personal."

"You were?"

"I'm ready to stop running, Russ. It's not worth it anymore." Her face moved closer to his. "Not without you."

"Are you sure? You know, we'll get all kinds of publicity. Everybody here knows who you are. And—"

"I know. And I've got to learn to live with it. But there's one thing I'll never learn to live with."

"What's that?"

"Losing you."

She kissed him, then—a long, slow, satisfying kiss that probably didn't have the seal of approval necessary for display in front of a bunch of teenagers. Russ didn't care. Apparently, neither did Jillian. She didn't end the kiss even when a raucous cheer rose up from the teens in the gym.

"Can I get that in a contract?" he asked softly when they came up for air.

"I was thinking of something long-term."

"Forty or fifty years?"

"At least. With an option to renew."

They kissed once more—just to seal the bargain.

HARLEQUIN®

Temptation®

the **Fortune Boys**

A funny, sexy miniseries from bestselling
author Elise Title!

**LOSING THEIR HEARTS MEANT
LOSING THEIR FORTUNES....**

If any of the four Fortune brothers were unfortunate enough to
wed, they'd be permanently divorced from the Fortune
millions—thanks to their father's last will and testament.

BUT CUPID HAD OTHER PLANS!
Meet Adam in #412 **ADAM & EVE** (Sept. 1992)
Meet Peter #416 **FOR THE LOVE OF PETE**
(Oct. 1992)
Meet Truman in #420 **TRUE LOVE** (Nov. 1992)
Meet Taylor in #424 **TAYLOR MADE** (Dec. 1992)

**WATCH THESE FOUR MEN TRY TO WIN
AT LOVE AND NOT FORFEIT $$$**

HARLEQUIN®

Temptation®

Rebels & Rogues

Alex: He was hot on the trail of a career-making story . . . until he was KO'd by a knockout—Gabriella.

THE MAVERICK
by Janice Kaiser
Temptation #417, November

All men are not created equal. Some are rough around the edges. Tough-minded but tenderhearted. Incredibly sexy. The tempting fulfillment of every woman's fantasy.

When it's time to fight for what they believe in, to win that special woman, our Rebels and Rogues are heroes at heart. Twelve Rebels and Rogues, one each month in 1992, only from Harlequin Temptation.

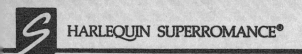

Take 4 bestselling love stories FREE

Plus get a FREE surprise gift!

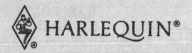

HARLEQUIN®

THE TAGGARTS OF TEXAS!

Harlequin's Ruth Jean Dale brings you
THE TAGGARTS OF TEXAS!

Those Taggart men—strong, sexy and hard to resist...

You've met Jesse James Taggart in FIREWORKS!
Harlequin Romance #3205 (July 1992)

Now meet Trey Smith—he's THE RED-BLOODED YANKEE!
Harlequin Temptation #413 (October 1992)

Then there's Daniel Boone Taggart in SHOWDOWN!
Harlequin Romance #3242 (January 1993)

And finally the Taggarts who started it all—in LEGEND!
Harlequin Historical #168 (April 1993)

Read all the Taggart romances!
Meet all the Taggart men!

Available wherever Harlequin books are sold.

If you missed *Fireworks!* (July 1992) and would like to order it, please send your name, address, zip or postal code, along with a check or money order for $2.89 (please do not send cash), plus 75¢ postage and handling ($1.00 in Canada) for each book ordered, payable to Harlequin Reader Service to:

In the U.S.

3010 Walden Avenue
P.O. Box 1325
Buffalo, NY 14269-1325

In Canada

P.O. Box 609
Fort Erie, Ontario
L2A 5X3

Please specify book title with your order.
Canadian residents add applicable federal and provincial taxes.